***Endorsements for* Milly for Mayor**

Milly for Mayor is a fun and refreshing romp in rural mid-America. As Mark Twain catalogued the speech of the South, Dorothy Ramsey captures the vernacular of the "fly-over states" in this story that will engage tweens and younger adolescents. Years of indifference about local politics has led to a static community milieu within which four pranksters launch a facetious write-in campaign to elect Milly to the mayoral office. When Milly wins, the surprising result is that active "grass-roots" participation results in positive and significant changes across the entire community. Parents of homeschoolers will particularly appreciate the frequent inclusion of mathematics as an integral part of planning and problem-solving, much like real life. Readers will certainly be looking forward to the next contribution by this budding new author.

—*Bruce Leeson, PhD, clinical psychologist*

One of the most valuable gifts any writer brings to the page is a vision of a better world. In *Milly for Mayor*, Dorothy Ramsey does just that. With her good-hearted romp through the politics of small-town life, Ramsey imagines for us a pleasing alternative to what we find reported in the news on any given day. The novella, set in a generic fictional Midwestern small town, opens on a cast of characters a little too happily entrenched in old habits and traditions. But when a practical joke during election season turns apathetic residents into actively engaged citizens, the entire community is transformed. *Milly for Mayor* can be seen as a parable, reminding readers that sometimes the world is what we make it. And if we want to make it a world where teenagers happily take to cleaning up parks and Chicken Drop Bingo is a thing, well, why not? If you can dream it, it just takes a little planning and a few willing hands to make it so.

—*Karen Shoemaker, author of* The Meaning of Names

Dorothy Ramsey's full-hearted embrace of Nebraska whimsy and good humor fill her book. The campaign she dreams up may be fictional, but we could do a lot worse than having her affectionate eye trained on real-life Washington.

—*Bob Greene, best-selling author*

MILLY
FOR
MAYOR

DOROTHY E. RAMSEY

Tropho Polis Publishing
Lincoln, Nebraska

© 2021 Dorothy E. Ramsey. All rights reserved.

No part of this publication may be reproduced, distributed, or transmitted in any form or by any means, including photocopying, recording, digital scanning, or other electronic or mechanical methods, without the prior written permission of the copyright holder, except in the case of brief quotations embodied in critical reviews and certain other noncommercial uses permitted by copyright law.

Tropho Polis Publishing
5109 Foxglove Circle
Lincoln, NE 68521

Printed in the United States of America

10 9 8 7 6 5 4 3 2 1
First Edition

ISBN: 978-1-7351274-0-8
Library of Congress Control Number: 2020909454

Editing, typesetting, and interior design
by Infusionmedia / https://infusion.media

Cover design by Rayna Collins

This book is dedicated to Rosie Gentry, who ran the B&M Café in Pleasant Hill, Missouri. The B&M Café, now long gone, is the inspiration for this story. This book is also dedicated to all the citizens who actually show up to vote on Election Day.

Contents

Preface vii
Acknowledgments ix

1	Chapter 1
11	Chapter 2
15	Chapter 3
23	Chapter 4
27	Chapter 5
31	Chapter 6
35	Chapter 7
39	Chapter 8
43	Chapter 9
55	Chapter 10
63	Chapter 11
69	Chapter 12
73	Chapter 13
79	Chapter 14
89	Chapter 15
101	Chapter 16
109	Chapter 17
113	Chapter 18
115	Chapter 19

121 Chapter 20
135 Chapter 21

Discussion Questions 147
About the Author 151

Preface

In the late 1980s/early 1990s, there was a little diner in Pleasant Hill called the B&M Café. Driving around looking for someplace for breakfast one weekend, my husband and I ventured out of Kansas City and found it, and we quickly made friends with the staff. I was waffling (no pun intended) on how to have my eggs cooked, and the server asked, "What's your favorite childhood memory of eggs for breakfast?" I described soft-boiled eggs mixed in with crumbled bacon and dry toast torn into bite-sized pieces; Mom called it Eggs in a Cup. When I described it, the server said, "Oh, yes, we have several who come in here and like their eggs that way. We call it Dan's Eggs, but it's not on the menu. I'll fix it like that for you." We went back for many Saturday breakfasts over the next few years, and they always remembered I liked Dan's Eggs.

My husband and I often played the game in airports or shopping mall food courts of speculating on the people we were seeing, what line of work they were in, or what they were talking about. One morning at the B&M Café, there were four gentlemen at the back table, in bib overalls and feed mill caps. I decided I thought they must be talking about the upcoming elections. As we drove home, we had this animated speculation on how we thought they'd vote and why. This story is the result.

That was some thirty years ago. I was recently driving home from across the state and happened to take a detour through Pleasant Hill. I decided to check out the B&M Café. Sadly, it's long gone; the building has been a closed-down antiques storefront for a while. I found another restaurant at the end of the block, clearly locally owned, and asked if anyone remembered the B&M Café. The cashier did, and she asked around, and one of the customers knew that the owner of the old place, Rosie Gentry, was in the town's nursing home, a few blocks away. (In Pleasant Hill, nothing is more than a few blocks away.) This manuscript was under construction, nearly done. I HAD to go see Rosie. She said she remembered us and fixing me Dan's Eggs, but I think she was just being polite. We had a great visit, and I told her I was writing a story where a location that plays a part in the story was based on her restaurant. Her eyes lit up, and she smiled an energized smile. I feel so lucky to have met her again just as this was coming to fruition.

Acknowledgments

This story would not have made it to fruition without the help of many smart, kind, and generous people who provided professional advice, suggestions, and encouragement throughout the process. Chief among them is Larry Ramsey, who though gone these twenty-some years, still encourages me to write. Equally gratifying is the consistent and somewhat unwarranted faith in me that is expressed by my daughter and grandsons. Mary Fischer contributed to the understanding of the election process from the other side of the voting booth. My brother, Braxton Mannar, lent a keen eye and Mom's profound love of the English language when he proofread. Mark VanOrder made time to read and critique and proofread and be my friend for twenty years. This story benefited greatly from the knowledge shared by David Shively, whose experience with election processes is vast, and he was generous with it. Cris and Aaron at Infusionmedia were invaluable in guiding me through the process after the pen was put to rest, and will be again. I'm sure I'm forgetting many individuals as I sit here, but to all who encouraged, taught, guided, pushed, and nagged me to finish this, I offer my sincerest thanks.

1

Jenny arrived at the café at five thirty a.m. sharp, just as she had for the last eighteen years. It was early January, so the sun was not even hinting at putting in an appearance. She shrugged out of her quilted winter coat and hung it on the hook beside the back door without even looking. "Good habits are good servants," her mother had often said. The habit of opening the café was so deeply ingrained, she wasn't even aware of her movements. The opening chores hadn't changed much in eighteen years. Jenny was glad of that—it left her mind free to ponder other things as she went about her opening rituals. She hit the light switches as if on autopilot. Soon the regulars would come in, and perhaps a new diner or two. There wasn't much that had changed in this little town, and when something did change, it was noticed and talked about for weeks. She erased yesterday's special from the wall board. Friday was always fried catfish. She wasn't sure she liked this new whiteboard and markers. She'd had a blackboard with white and pink chalk for the first sixteen years, and it had been good enough. The whiteboard had been rescued when the school remodeled some classrooms. Most of the residents from the town itself as well as the surrounding farms weren't big on fixing what wasn't broken. But times change, even in rural Midwest farm towns, and customers seemed to like this one OK. They didn't even mention that it was different anymore. Saturday's special was always meat loaf, from her grandmother's recipe, with mashed potatoes and peas, frozen last summer from her garden at home. The markers squeaked as she wrote, but it wasn't the same sound as chalk.

It was hard to believe in mid-January that the sun was coming up earlier these days. It was still dark out, but Jenny's Café would open in about twenty minutes, so she hurried to get coffee ready to brew, lots of eggs, bacon, and ham ready for orders. She started a big pan of grits and cubed some potatoes to cook with onion and peppers on the grill. At six thirty sharp, she unlocked the front door and turned on the electric "OPEN" sign in the window. Another one of Patsy's new ideas—the old one had been a piece of thin wood with "OPEN" printed on one side and "CLOSED" on the other that hung on a nail by a length of twine. Jenny had no idea as she opened for business that this morning, in this café, wheels would be put in motion that would change the town forever.

The small rural farm community that surrounded Bridgeford had a slightly different rhythm on Saturday mornings. There were still early morning chores—there always are when animals are involved—but on Saturday, many of the locals had breakfast at Jenny's instead of at home. The door opened, and the little bell at the top jingled. At least that's still the same, she thought. She liked that bell. Jenny turned to see Ralph and Dan making their way to their usual table at the back. "Coffee and orange juice to start, boys?"

"I'll have tomato juice this morning," Dan replied, unzipping his winter coat. He hung it across the back of his chair and sat down.

"You're just a wild and crazy guy, Dan Harless," she said, and she brought the coffeepot to the table, righted the overturned cups, and filled them. She was pouring the juice when Steve and Johnny Ray came in.

"Coffee and OJ, Jenny," Steve called out as he made his way back to join his friends.

"Me too," Johnny Ray added.

The four longtime friends gave her their breakfast orders, and she started the food on the grill. They looked like they got their denim bib overalls from the same local discount store and their ball caps at the same feed store. They were all between forty-five and fifty years old and had lived in Bridgeford all their lives.

At seven o'clock, Patsy arrived to help Jenny with the growing breakfast crowd. Unlike Jenny, who wore her usual white nylon waitress dress and black apron, Patsy was a newer employee. Ten years ago, she had showed up in slacks and a button-down blouse, and she hadn't worn an apron once since she started. The whiteboard and electric open sign had been her ideas.

"Hey, boys," she said as she made her way to the back room to deposit her purse on a shelf and hang her coat on the hook next to Jenny's.

"Hey, Patsy," they chorused. Dan caught her eye and continued, "It's coming up election time in April, that's only nine weeks away. How come there aren't any campaign flyers in the window?"

"Well, I guess there's no need. Everybody knows Arthur Linden is going to win. He's the only one even running," she replied. "He would win if you four were the only voters to show up."

"True enough, I guess," Dan replied. "And there probably won't be more than that who bother to vote anyway."

"Well, there's not much mayoring that needs to be done, and what little there is, Arthur seems to get it done," Steve offered.

"You're right about that," Ralph chimed in. "It's a part-time job at best, and Arthur only mayors for part of that."

Just then, the little copper cowbell above the door jingled again, and a young man dressed in khakis and a pullover shirt came in, accompanied by a young woman his own age. They paused inside the door and looked around. When he saw Dan and the others at the back table, he made his way toward them. "Uncle Dan, I was betting I'd find you here on Saturday morning."

"Jason, what brings you to town this morning? Have a seat." Dan pulled his chair back from the table, and Steve got up to help him slide another table alongside theirs. Dan sat and moved his coffee to his new place at the table. He spoke as he arranged his coffee and juice. "Who's your friend? Jenny, bring these young folks some coffee and orange juice. Guys, this is my nephew Jason. You remember him, my brother Henry's boy. He used to come and help on the farm in summers. He's in college now up north."

They all welcomed Jason and his friend, and they took a seat at the table. "Uncle Dan, this is

Stephanie Mannar. We're both studying political science."

The men all greeted Stephanie. "You gentlemen are discussing weather and hogs, right?" she asked with a friendly grin.

"You got us pegged pretty good for a usual Saturday, Stephanie. But not today. Today we're talking about the mayor's race," Steve replied.

"Well, it's not really a race because he's uncontested," Johnny Ray chimed in. "He could walk backwards instead of running, and he'd still win."

Dan smiled at her. "And nobody bothers to vote because we all know he's automatic, and he won't do much of anything anyway. He hasn't the last twelve years he's been mayor. Just shows up at parades and so forth. I'd actually vote for anybody else just for the change. Wouldn't take much to do nothing but what Arthur does."

Ralph sipped his coffee. He got a conspiratorial look in his eye. "Heck, Dan, your damn mule could do as much mayoring as Arthur does, and probably do a better job of doing nothing."

Dan shook his head even while he was laughing. He'd seen that look in Ralph's eye before. "Ralph, a mule can't run for mayor."

"Why not? He was born here, so he's a citizen, and since the city annexed up to the highway, your place is in the city now, so he's a resident." Ralph's eyes were twinkling as he goaded his old friend.

"Because the mule's not on the ballot, for one thing," Dan replied.

Steve was catching the fun of it and winked at Ralph. "You could put him on the ballot."

"Uncle Dan," Jason spoke up, "I've only had one semester of political science, but I'm pretty sure you can't put a mule on the ballot. He can't sign his name on the paperwork."

"True enough. See, guys? You can't put a mule on the ballot. Thank you, son," he nodded emphatically at Jason.

"I still like the idea, I think it's funny," Steve said. "I wish we could put him on the ballot. I'd vote for him just for a laugh."

"You sure he can't be added to the ballot, Jason?" Johnny Ray asked.

Jason looked around the table and a sliver of mischief seemed to take hold of him. He looked over at Stephanie with a raised eyebrow that said, 'Should I go for it?' and Stephanie, who clearly knew that look, grinned impishly and shrugged her shoulders. Jason looked back at his uncle and with a measured drawl said, "Well, the deadline for registering has already passed anyway, so it doesn't matter. He can't be put on the ballot.

But..." he hesitated. Stephanie nodded her encouragement at him, and he continued, "He could always be a write-in if the four of you want to do it."

Ralph put some strawberry jam on his toast. He looked up. "I'm gonna do it. I'm gonna write in your damn mule. What's his name?"

"Well, for one thing, he's not a he, he's a she. Her name is Milly. But you can't just write in Milly, you fool," Dan said.

"Well, she's your mule, so her full name is Milly Harless. I'm writing her in." He looked expectantly around the table. "You guys in or not?"

They all looked at Ralph. He took a bite of toast and looked right back at them. He tugged the bill of his cap with determination. "You guys wouldn't know how to have an adventure if it bit you in the butt. Y'all are just gettin' old, I guess." It was not the first time he had dared them to do something.

Not one to be challenged and walk away, Steve spoke next. "I'm in," he said. "If this is your idea of an adventure, what harm can it do? She can't win, and we can have a laugh over it later with Arthur."

"I'm in," Johnny Ray said. "Milly Harless for Mayor. Come on, Dan, you gotta see the fun in this."

"Oh, for crying out loud, you guys are crazy." He looked around the table at his three friends.

They had pulled pranks in high school, but that was years ago, and they were adults now. Adults don't have time to pull pranks. There's work to be done. He looked at Jason. "This is all your fault."

"Not me," Jason replied, grinning as he gave a quick wink to Stephanie. "I just answered a few questions. This is Ralph's idea."

Dan looked back at his friends. "Well. OK, because she'll only get four votes. You guys are crazy."

2

The next Saturday, the four friends gathered again for breakfast at Jenny's Café. Steve had carried a paper bag in with him, which he had slipped under his chair when he arrived. As they ate, he reached below, retrieved the bag, and laid it flat on the table, giving it a congratulatory pat. "Got something for you guys," he said as he put catsup on his hash browns. "Had to go to Velka City this week, so I stopped at one of those quick-print shops."

"Well, don't keep us in suspense here. What is it?" Dan asked.

Steve took a bite of hash browns. "Hold your horses, Dan, I don't want this food to go cold." But he put his fork down and reached inside the bag. When he withdrew his hand, he was holding a stack of papers. He handed a page from the stack to each of his friends. "They're campaign posters for Milly," he said. "I figured we could let some of the rest of the town in on our fun."

They looked at the paper he had handed them. A standard sheet of typing paper, it had printed on it: "Let's get it *write*" across the top in big letters. Down from that was "Latecomer Milly Harless would make a great mayor of Bridgeford but is not on the ballot. She's agreed to serve if elected, so let's all write her in." And at the bottom, in huge black block letters, "WRITE IN MILLY HARLESS FOR MAYOR" with a small tagline "Paid for by the Milly for Mayor Committee."

Johnny Ray spoke first. "Who's the Milly for Mayor Committee?"

"Well," Steve said, "so far, it's just me since I paid for the printing. But the committee welcomes all interested parties, if you guys want to chip in."

"I'll split it with you," Ralph grinned.

"Me too," Johnny Ray said.

They all looked at Dan. "I'm providing her room and board, any medical care, and all her education."

Steve laughed. "Fair enough. You're on the committee too, Dan. In fact, you guys don't have to pay anything either." He looked at Ralph and Johnny Ray. "It wasn't all that expensive, and this is gonna be fun. But the rules are, we won't tell anyone that Milly is a mule. Let them think whatever they want. If they ask who she is, we just say we're not sure, but she could be that young lady that came to town with Jason Harless, Dan's nephew. Let's see how far we can take this."

Dan shook his head in amusement. "You are crazy. This will never work."

"So no harm, no foul. Let's just see how far it can go," Ralph countered.

"We can start right here," Steve said. "Hey, Jenny, come here a minute." She brought a full coffeepot to refill their cups. Steve looked at her with an earnest, hopeful gaze. "Do you mind if we put this poster in the front window? Milly's staying out at the Harless place, and she'll be here for a while, and we talked her into trying for mayor."

"Really? Instead of Arthur?" She shrugged. "I don't care. Go ahead. I don't know what Arthur does besides show up at parades, anyway. She doesn't have to be a longtime resident to do that." Jenny took a flyer and taped it to the front plate-glass window right by the door.

The four friends finished their breakfast, and each took a portion of the stack of flyers. "Now, we'll each take a section of town and see how many of these we can get on display. We'll use Main and Oak as the crossroads. Johnny Ray, you live up by the new supermarket, so you take the northwest section. I'll take northeast, with the bank. Ralph, you can take the southeast section of the town, and Dan, you take the southwest part. We'll each see how much of our section we can get to promote Milly. That sound like a plan?"

"Works for me," Johnny Ray said. "My barber is in that area. I'll start with him."

"I can start at Miller's Hardware," Ralph agreed. "And the feed store is real close to that."

"I suppose I can get Food-Rite and the drugstore" Dan said. "And maybe a few other offices like maybe my insurance guy, Howard Strawson. I've got to go see him anyway."

"This will be great fun. I've got the furniture store and the bar on Eighth Street. We've got eleven weeks." Steve was clearly going to be the leader of this Milly for Mayor Committee.

3

That next Thursday night, Jenny arrived at Amanda's Beauty Parlor for her usual Thursday night appointment. She settled into the chair, and Amanda draped a smock around her neck. "Say, Jenny, what's up with the poster in your window for Milly Harless for Mayor. Who is she?"

Jenny shrugged under the cape. "I think she's Dan's nephew's wife. They asked me to put it up last Saturday, a week after they were in the café having breakfast with Dan and his friends."

SueEllen in the next chair spoke up. "I remember his nephew; used to come work on the farm on Saturdays. Do they live in Bridgeford now?"

Jenny turned to answer SueEllen, and Amanda turned her head back to face the mirror. "Sit still or I'll cut your hair wrong," she chided.

Jenny slid her eyes toward SueEllen. "I don't know, but they probably live somewhere close if she's running for mayor."

"Wonder why she'd want to do that?" SueEllen said.

"Maybe she figures it wouldn't take much time, and it'd be a way to get to know people. If she's new in town, she might feel kind of isolated if she doesn't get a job or make friends somehow." Jenny thought a minute. "It's actually not a bad idea, maybe some fresh ideas from a younger person." Then she laughed. "I can't believe I just said that, as much as I resisted Patsy's fresh ideas at the café!"

"Well, if they have any extras, they can put a flyer in my window. I'll chat her up, maybe she'll come in here to get her hair done. You want some light color on your hair, Jenny?"

"Sure, maybe some highlights or something. I'll tell the boys to bring you a flyer when I see them Saturday." Jenny smiled at her reflection in the mirror. She couldn't believe she was advocating for a change in the town's mayor, but she didn't want Patsy to get all the credit for progress around here.

Later that afternoon, Ralph stepped into Miller's Hardware and picked up some birdseed, some shelf brackets, and a new stepladder. Bill Miller approached his friend with a welcoming smile. "Hey, Ralph, let me help you carry some of that."

"Thanks, Bill," Ralph replied. "That darn ladder you sold me fifteen years ago gave out, so I guess I need a new one."

They both laughed. "Well, it was only guaranteed for fourteen years, so I guess you got your money's worth. Need anything else?" They were approaching the checkout counter.

"Well, now that you mention it, I do. Not something to buy, but a favor. A friend of mine has a relative who wants to run for mayor." He couldn't help but smile as he thought of the look on Dan's face when he told him he had referred to Milly as his relative. "I've got some flyers for her in the truck. Can I bring one in for your front window?"

"Instead of Arthur? Ain't nobody run against him in at least a decade," he mused. "Sure, bring one in. Can't hurt to give old Arthur something to think about."

"Thanks." Ralph paid for his purchases, and Bill helped him carry the ladder to the truck. Ralph reached into the truck and retrieved one of the flyers.

"Who's on the committee here?" Bill was pointing to the bottom line of the flyer. "We haven't had anything sound so formal in Bridgeford for a long time."

"Well, it's me, Dan, Johnny Ray, and Steve. I think you know all of them."

"Why don't you give me another—I'll put one on each side of the door," Bill said.

"Thanks, Bill." Ralph handed him two more flyers. "Here's one more than that, in case you know somebody who would help."

That same week, Johnny Ray was getting his biweekly trim. Sam had been cutting Johnny Ray's hair since he was six years old, and like many, his cut had not changed much in that time. The flattop was a little thinner, and some gray was starting to show, but he'd had his hair like this so long, it never even occurred to him to change it. It was ten minutes twice a month, trouble-free. But he did enjoy hanging around afterward to chat with friends who had "high-maintenance" hairstyles. "Sam, you gonna vote for Milly?" he asked.

"Son, I haven't bothered to vote in twenty years. One person can't make a difference, for one thing, and Arthur's been mayor for so long now, it's obvious he'll be mayor as long as he wants to."

"Likely you're right," Johnny Ray continued. "But it would be interesting to see what would happen in this old town if somebody else won."

"Not interesting enough for me to stand in some line after work. I stand on my feet all day long, and by the end of the day, I want to go home, sit back in my recliner, and watch some TV. Besides, you know Arthur will win, he always does."

Bruce chimed in. "I think so too. I've known Arthur a long time, and he knows what to do. This new gal won't know nothing about what to do."

"So, are you voting for Arthur then?" Johnny Ray asked.

"If I'm in town on Election Day, I'll probably vote for him. But if that's a day I have an out-of-town delivery, I won't worry about it. I usually don't come back in after an out-of-town delivery."

"I can sure understand that," Johnny Ray agreed. "Sometimes I have to come in after a full day on the farm, and it seems like a whole 'nother day of work after I've worked all day. But, Sam, you don't care if I put a flyer in your window, do you? It would sure get a lot of people to see it. Everybody needs a haircut, right?"

"I don't care. You can put as many flyers in the window as you want. Makes no difference to me. That'll be seven fifty for the haircut."

"Thanks, buddy. See you in two weeks." Johnny Ray handed Sam a ten-dollar bill, taped a flyer to the inside of Sam's window, and waved as he left.

The next Saturday, the Milly for Mayor Committee was settling into their breakfast, and each shared where they had placed posters. Dan, still skeptical, said, "Didn't anybody question who Milly is?"

Ralph answered first. "I just told them she might be your relative. Nobody acted like it made any difference who it was." He caught Dan's expression at the mention of relative and was glad he had practiced keeping an innocent look on his face.

Johnny Ray nodded his head. "Same here. Mostly they all said 'sure' when I asked and didn't even pay attention to what I was asking. I got six of them put out in my quadrant."

Steve sat up taller and squared his shoulders proudly. "Your *quadrant?* You got a *quadrant?* I got fifteen out in my *quadrant.*"

"Well, no doubt," Ralph said. "You gave yourself the business district with more windows."

Steve took no offense; these four had been jibing each other since elementary school.

Ralph took a gulp of coffee and said, "I didn't count. I guess I got maybe a dozen. Were we supposed to count and report back?"

"I hope not," Dan shook his head. "I didn't do that many."

"No matter," said Steve. "Just keep them on hand and put them in places when you can. Remember, it's all just in fun."

4

It was Friday morning, and the payday shoppers were at Food-Rite getting their weekly groceries. Arthur Linden was about to reach for a gallon of milk when Amanda approached. "Good morning, Arthur. How are you doing today?" she greeted the mayor.

"I'm fine as frog hair, fine as frog hair," Arthur replied. "Keeping yourself busy, Amanda?"

"Yep, shop's doing well, and the kids are growing up. Can't complain."

Arthur put the milk in his basket. "I remember when I was first elected mayor, those kids weren't even born yet. I bet they're in middle school now."

"One is, the other will be next year," Amanda replied. "Speaking of mayor, are you worried about that write-in candidate, Milly Harless?"

"What write-in candidate? I don't know about any write-in candidate. I had the town clerk check the ballot before it was printed, and I'm the only one running again."

"I know. There's a bunch of posters going up across town for a write-in vote for her. I'm surprised you haven't seen them." They pushed their baskets toward the front.

"Well, there can't be too many. I haven't seen any," Arthur replied. "Besides, I've been mayor for twelve years now, and I can't believe some new woman I never heard of has a chance. Nothing to worry about." He gave her a condescending smile. As he finished paying and left the store, Arthur didn't notice Dan Harless coming into the market with a sheaf of flyers in his hand.

By the next week, the word had spread even further. The Ditzy Dozen was gathered at Amanda's house. It was Tuesday night, and her bridge friends were showing up for their weekly game. Three card tables were set up in the parlor, and there were a few bottles of wine and various cheeses and fruits on one platter and a selection of cupcakes on another. Her husband, John, had started the group's name when he came home from poker night early and found the ladies slightly inebriated and laughing together. "Well, here we have the ditzy dozen for sure," he had remarked, and the name stuck.

Tonight, the conversation was jovial but not as frivolous as usual. "Hey, Amanda, I saw the poster in your window. Who's Milly Harless?" one of the ladies asked.

Amanda set out a plate of deviled eggs. "You know Jenny from the café? I do her hair, and she brought it over. Says she thinks it's a relative of Dan Harless. I don't think I remember meeting her. I know I've never done her hair."

"I wonder what she's like, and why she would want to be mayor," Margaret from the same table spoke up.

"I don't know, but it wouldn't hurt to have more women in politics," Betsy offered her opinion.

"I don't know if you could call being mayor of Bridgeport 'in politics' exactly," Margaret replied. "We're not exactly a hotbed of political action."

"That's true, but it wouldn't take much to do more than Arthur's done. No offense, Lucy. I know he's your brother."

Lucy looked up from studying her cards. "None taken. He wasn't a go-getter when he was fourteen years old, either. I had to do most of his chores or we'd have never gotten to go to the movies."

"Do you think she has a chance?" This was Betsy again.

"Well, we could maybe help her. We could be like a lobby or something and help spread the word to get our friends involved," Amanda answered.

"I can ask the other teachers if they've seen the posters," Margaret piped up.

"It would be kind of interesting to see what would be different with a new mayor," Amanda said.

Each of the women agreed to help spread the word that there could be a new mayor if they all wrote in Milly's name. What could it hurt? Only Lucy said, "I'll help spread the word, but I really think I'd have to vote for Arthur, him being family and all."

"It's a secret ballot, Lucy. Vote for whoever you want to. Let Arthur assume what he needs to."

"It's OK, she can vote for Arthur," her partner spoke up for her.

Lucy looked uncertain, remembering the chores she had done for him as a child so they could go to the movies. "He got to go to a lot of Weekend Westerns because I washed dishes when it was his turn," she mused, mostly to herself.

The ladies refreshed their drinks and continued their games. The conversation turned to the latest movie stars' escapades.

5

It was Tuesday, a week before the election, and Arthur Linden was getting worried. His brow was furrowed in thought as he entered the PrintQuick in Velka City. He still hadn't met this Milly person, but there sure were a lot of her posters showing up around town. Even worse, a few people were starting to kid him about what he would be doing after the election, with all his extra time.

"Can I help you?" the young lady at the counter asked.

"Yes, I think you can," Arthur responded. "I've got some business across the street for about an hour and I wonder if I drop this off with you, could I pick up fifty copies in a little while?" He handed her the page with "VOTE FOR ARTHUR LINDEN" at the top, a picture of him that obviously was not recent, and "A MAYOR WITH EXPERIENCE" across the bottom.

"We can do that," she responded. "Your name?"

Arthur looked startled for minute. "I'm Arthur Linden. That's my picture there."

"Oh, of course," she grinned sheepishly. "What was I thinking? I'll have them ready for you in just a little while."

"Thanks," Arthur said.

A short time later, he'd finished with his dentist appointment and came back to get his flyers. As he drove back to Bridgeford, he tried to stop himself from worrying. He called his wife once he was on the highway. "I'm not worried, Sarah," he said. "Write-in candidates never win, but I don't like seeing all those posters—somebody might think I'm not running."

"Don't worry, Arthur. You've been mayor for three terms now, you'll be mayor again. I know I don't know much about politics, but I haven't heard anyone say they're voting for that other lady. I don't even know who she is."

He knew Sarah's support was born more of loyalty than knowledge, but he felt better talking to her. He patted the pile of posters beside him in the seat. "Thanks, babe. I'm almost to the crossroad. I'll be home soon." He drove the rest of the way back, outlining in his mind the places he'd seen Milly's poster and planning how he could get one of his beside each one of hers. By the time he got home, he had stopped worrying and was thinking about the ball game that would be on TV later that evening.

6

It was Election Day, the polls were officially closed, and Jenny couldn't remember when the café had been this busy. She had let customers know they were welcome to stay after dinner to watch the election returns together. A television was perched on top of a tall bookshelf on the back wall. Now past the usual closing time of eight p.m., she had desserts and coffee ready, and the banter was friendly with a sporadic hush as the results were broadcast every fifteen to twenty minutes. Bridgeford didn't get much attention. Most of the results were for the larger cities in the state, but occasionally a scroll at the bottom of the screen showed local results as they were counted. It was nine thirty when the news announcer's voice hushed the room. "In the small town of Bridgeford, all ballots are in." The patrons immediately shushed each other. The announcer continued, "A dark horse, Milly Harless, a write-in candidate, has upset longtime incumbent Arthur Linden for mayor." All faces turned to look at Arthur, who was staring at the screen with his mouth hanging open in surprise.

"What? You've got to be kidding me," he stammered.

The announcer was still talking. "The turnout surprised the vote counters tonight as ballots came in. Seems there was a larger turnout than in past elections by 11 percent. This small town of 1,433 registered voters typically has about 38 percent of their registered voters who show up at the polls. Tonight, there were 702 votes, 267 for Arthur Linden and 435 for Milly Harless."

In the back at their regular table, Milly's campaign committee stared at each other. The crowd was laughing and clapping each other on the back. Someone shouted, "Speech, speech." "Where is she, anyway? She should make a speech."

Dan still looked too startled to respond. Steve spoke up. "She's not here," he stammered. "She really didn't expect to win."

"It was supposed to be a joke," Dan said, but no one heard him. "How did this happen? Now what do we do?" He looked at Ralph.

Ralph and Steve were laughing and slapping the table. "We did it! We did it," they said back and forth. Johnny Ray looked at them, and at Dan, and just shrugged, but his grin was wide and his eyes were laughing.

7

Dan was just finishing up the early morning farm chores when a blue sedan pulled into the drive. He brushed his hands against his overalls, adjusted the brim of his cap, and squinted—he didn't recognize the man who shut the car door and started walking toward him. "Mr. Harless?"

"Yes, that's me," Dan replied. "What can I do for you?"

"I'm Stan Cottner, from the *Velka City Sentinel*. I'd like to interview Milly Harless. I understand from folks in town she lives here, or near here?"

Dan's first thought was to strangle his friends at next Saturday's breakfast. "Um, she's not available right now. What exactly did you want to ask?"

"Oh, the usual profile things: how long has she lived in the community, how long has she wanted to be in politics. I asked around in town this morning, and people in town didn't seem to know much about her. That's interesting to our readers—an unknown winning as a write-in candidate."

"Yes," Dan mused. "Yes, I suppose that is unusual."

Stan got a small notebook from his pocket. "You know her pretty well, do you?" he asked.

"I guess you could say that." Dan was thinking fast. How long could he get away with this?

"Someone said they thought she was married to your nephew Jason?" Stan prompted.

"No, actually they just happen to have the same last name. It's sort of a coincidence, I guess." Dan kept his expression blank as best he could.

"How long has she been interested in politics?" Stan pressed.

"Oh, it's a fairly recent thing, I think." Dan looked off to the horizon as if preoccupied with the weather.

"What are her qualifications?" Stan asked.

"I really think you need to ask her these questions. I'm not sure I should be speaking for her. As I said, she's not available right now. But I can take your phone number if you want."

Stan was not pleased but tried one more time. "Do you have a picture of her we can run?"

"No, I don't remember seeing a picture of her in the last few years." Dan was feeling lucky to have made up a plausible response to each question so far but was really wishing Stan would leave. "I've got to leave pretty soon for an appointment. Like I said, if you want to leave your number..." He let the rest trail off without making any commitment regarding what he would do with it.

Stan fished in his pocket for a business card. "Here you go. If you'd ask her to call me at her earliest convenience, I'd really appreciate it."

"I promise," Dan said with a smile. He would certainly be glad to ask. He didn't promise a response. Then inspiration struck. "You know, the swearing-in is a week from Saturday. You can print that this week, then could come with your photographer, and it would be a great story. You could ask her all your questions then." Thinking on his feet with no idea if he could make his wild thoughts come true, he continued, "It will be right across the street from the City Hall." He said this with a conviction he didn't feel. There was an empty building where the old bus station had been, when the bus line still had scheduled stops in Bridgeford.

Stan got into his car and drove off, unsatisfied. He hadn't reached the highway before Dan was on the phone to Ralph. "What are we going to do now? You started this, and I just committed to a swearing-in ceremony a week from Saturday at the old bus station."

Ralph laughed until his eyes watered. "Well then, I guess we gotta go get it ready before then.

I'll call Steve and Johnny Ray. We can set it up this week. We do have to let people know..."

"I told that reporter, his name is Stan something, I told him to put in the paper that the swearing-in is a week from Saturday across from the City Hall."

Ralph laughed again. "Dan, you're a natural. See? You're great at this!"

"You know we can't keep this up, don't you? You know a mule can't really be mayor, don't you?"

"I don't know any such thing. Milly got elected fair and square. Milly's gonna be the mayor. See you Saturday." Ralph hung up before Dan could protest any more.

8

The Milly for Mayor Committee gathered for their Saturday breakfast, and Steve waved the *Velka City Sentinel* in the air. "Look at this!" he exclaimed. "Milly made the news!" He folded the newspaper open and pointed to the headline: "MILLY HARLESS TO BE SWORN IN AS MAYOR OF BRIDGEFORD."

Ralph read the short article aloud for his friends. "The reporter is Stan Cottner. The article says, 'Milly Harless, in an unexpected upset, has won the election for mayor in Bridgeford as a write-in candidate. She will be sworn in next Saturday across from the City Hall. She was not available for comment at press time, but past Mayor Arthur Linden said he did not know who she was, and she was not on the ballot. She won with write-in votes. The Sentinel will be on hand Saturday to interview her and will run more information in two weeks.'"

Dan looked pleased with himself. "That young reporter fella came by the farm last week, and I had no idea what to say to him, but I didn't let him see Milly and told him if he'd give me his number, I'd ask her to call him. I did ask her, but she didn't seem to care."

Johnny Ray wiped the toast crumbs from his face. "I guess the article two weeks from now is going to be a little different," he offered dryly.

Ralph finished chewing and took up the conversation. "Dan called me right after this Cottner guy left. He and I are going to put up a sort of a stage in front of the old bus station across from City Hall. We figure we can bring her out from behind the station and up on stage, and let people see her. Dan can read her the oath, and we can only hope she nods her head." He grinned as he stopped to sip some coffee. "I can't wait to see people's faces, especially Arthur."

"I've got lumber left from when I added that extra shed on my place. I'll bring it," Steve offered.

"Maybe you can get the mayor's budget to reimburse you for the new mayor's office. She can come to town for official office hours every Saturday," Ralph said.

Dan shook his head. "I don't want any part of any city money mixed up with this. This will all fall apart at some point, and I don't want anything to do with city money attached to it."

"You've got a good point there, Dan." Ralph nodded. "We'll borrow some folding chairs from the dance hall, and people can sit and clap. That reporter can take pictures. I'll have a hay bale or two on the stage for her."

"So, you guys all show up Thursday. It shouldn't take more than two days to build this," Johnny Ray said. "I'll check with Sam at the barbershop. I think the bus station rented the space from him. He probably still owns it."

And with that, the swearing-in ceremony was assured.

9

Saturday was a beautiful spring day, with a few clouds to punctuate the sky, bringing shade but not rain. It was the kind of day that would make any April proud. The lawn of the bus station had folding chairs that once were white but now were gray with age. Dan had arrived earlier in the day with Milly in a horse trailer and parked it in the bus-loading lanes out of sight. At the curb facing the front of the station, the men had erected a small stage with a lectern and bunting banners in patriotic red, white, and blue strung across the top. Steve had brought some Memorial Day bunting to put along the front of the raised stage edge. Because they had no further use for them, they stapled the undistributed flyers to the front of the lectern. With rudimentary steps on one side and a ramp on the other side, they thought the photo op was perfect, with the City Hall's prominent sign and distinctive profile right across the street. Steve had posted temporary "NO PARKING" signs along the curb to keep the view open. Johnny Ray placed a bale of hay near the lectern.

It was almost eleven thirty, and people would be gathering pretty soon. Stan Cottner pulled up, parked in the closest space, and recognized Dan. Another man was with him, carrying a camera with an impressively long lens. Dan grinned at his friends. "Are we ready for this?"

The other three nodded enthusiastically. As Stan and his colleague approached the four friends, Dan stepped out to greet them. "Stan, I saw that article you wrote for us. I hope it helps to bring out a good crowd for the swearing-in."

Stan nodded. "Thanks! Good morning, gentlemen. This is Alex Stevens. He's a photographer with the *Sentinel*."

Dan continued, "This is Steve Gespie, Johnny Ray Reynolds, and Ralph Wightman, the rest of the Milly for Mayor Committee." He nodded at each man in turn. Stan and Alex shook hands with each man.

"Would it be possible to have a brief interview with Ms. Harless before the swearing-in?" Stan asked.

Dan spoke first. "Well, perhaps afterward would be better. We've got kind of a different type of swearing-in ceremony planned, and you'll probably be better prepared to talk to her afterward." Ralph suppressed a chuckle. His once-reluctant friend was getting good at this! Dan pointed to Arthur Linden who was just arriving. "That's our current mayor, Arthur Linden, who lost to Milly. You might want to speak to him a bit while you wait, for historical insight or perspective or something."

Stan started to object, but Ralph spoke up. "Stan, I was meaning to ask you. I noticed you take notes on a little notepad. Don't you reporter fellas mostly use tape recorders? Why are you taking notes on a little notepad like in the 1940s movies?"

Stan smiled wide, and his eyes lit up. "You know, Ralph, most people don't even pay attention to that. I'm impressed you noticed. Actually, my grandfather was a reporter for the *Chicago Tribune* back in his day, and I was always a little starstruck. I thought being a reporter for a newspaper must be the most exciting, romantic, and dashing thing a fella could do." He closed the notepad and showed Ralph the initials in the corner. "My grandfather's initials," he said, pointing. "My grandfather could tell stories of all the events he covered, fires, elections, and other things. My brother and I would listen after dinners to all his adventures. When he died, Grandma told me he left me this notepad cover, and I used it all through college, and now I'm using it when I cover stories, just like he did."

"That's wonderful," Ralph said with genuine warmth in his voice. "It probably makes you feel more connected to him and all."

"Yep, plus I don't have to listen to all the 'in-between' time that a tape recorder would include. I write directly from my notes."

Just then, Jenny walked up. "Excuse me, gentlemen, but I need to speak to whoever is in charge of the ceremony. Dan, would that be you?"

Glad to escape Stan's persistence, Dan turned to Stan. "Thanks again for being here. I'll talk to you later." When he and Jenny had walked a few steps away, he said, "What's up, Jenny?"

"Well, people have been talking, and because Milly's an unknown and people are curious, I think you're going to have a lot of people here. Look." She pointed down to the corner. "People are starting to show up already. What would you think if I set up a small concession stand and sold coffee and tea and some easy sandwiches? I could serve chicken salad and a loaf of bread, make 'em on the spot."

"I think that would be great, Jenny," he replied. "You may have overheard me telling that newsman that the swearing-in will be a little different than last time, so people may hang around afterward. Having a bite of food for them is a great idea. And it's only right it should come from you—your place was practically Milly's campaign headquarters."

"Great. Thanks, Dan. I just happen to have a card table and a cooler and some paper plates in the car. I took the liberty ... I thought you might say yes. I'll be ready soon."

More people were beginning to arrive and seat themselves in small groups. Arthur Linden was sitting in the back row, and people were gathered around him, swearing they didn't know how this happened. They each assured him they had voted for him. "Well, it was a close race, and the people have spoken, so I'm here to congratulate the winner and offer any assistance and experience I can." Stan came over and started asking questions that were clearly going to result in a review of the accomplishments of Arthur's long run as mayor.

"I guess Arthur's going to find some way to be tooting his own horn, even at the opponent's swearing-in ceremony." Johnny Ray shook his head.

Ralph laughed. "Well, it's gonna be a short article then 'cause there's not all that much to say about that."

By now the gray chairs were full, and some people were bringing folding lawn chairs from their cars. It was almost noon, and Jenny was almost through setting up "Jenny's Sidewalk Café" at the back corner by the bus station's big front window.

Ralph caught the eye of his three friends. They all gave him the go-ahead nod. Dan turned to go into the bus station. Ralph strode up to the stage, mounted the stairs, and crossed to the lectern. He raised his hands to quell the chatter. "Ladies and gentlemen, I'm Ralph Wightman. Welcome to the swearing-in of Milly Harless as our new mayor. We weren't expecting such a big turnout, and we don't have any sound system set up, so I'm just going to talk loud."

The crowd nodded and a few clapped. Someone in the back hollered, "That's fine, Ralph. We can hear you back here."

Ralph looked toward the bus station. "As you all know, Milly was a write-in candidate, and I can tell you, those of us on her campaign team never dreamed she'd win. We were astounded. But here we are, maybe the first time a write-in candidate has ever won an election. We'll have to have Stan here from the newspaper check that out." He pointed to Stan in the front row. "Folks, this here is Stan Cottner, from the *Sentinel*, and his photographer friend Alex. Be nice to them. They're going to write all about our little town." Stan and Alexander each raised a hand and gave a short wave in response.

Jenny, just putting the menu and price list on her table, was turned toward the big front window of the bus station. She was the first to see Dan leading Milly through the station and the open front door. Only those closest to her in the back row heard her gasp of surprise. Ralph saw Dan and Milly emerge and said, "Ladies and gentlemen, with no further ado, I present for her swearing-in as mayor of Bridgeford, Milly Harless."

By now, Dan and Milly had reached the back row and were proceeding up the aisle in the middle of the chairs. Arthur's gasp of surprise was much louder than Jenny's had been. It was enough to get everyone to turn and look. Milly, with a rope halter and a ten-foot lead, was making her way to the front, across to the ramp, and up to the center of the stage.

"What's this?" Arthur bellowed. "Where's Milly Harless? What's that mule doing here?"

Ralph raised his hands again to hush the murmur that was rising from the lawn. Stan was scribbling furiously in his notebook. Alex was firing off the camera as quickly as he could. "Quiet, please.

Quiet, everyone. We can explain everything." The chatter quieted some. "Steve, Johnny Ray, come on up here."

When the four were standing on stage, with Milly in the center, Ralph continued, "Quiet, quiet, please, folks. I know if you just listen quietly for a little bit, we can be heard without yelling." Various members of the audience shushed each other, the crowd settled down, and Ralph nodded at Dan.

"Most of you know me. I'm Dan Harless, and I'm one of the four who were the campaign committee for Milly." At the sound of her name from her owner, Milly bobbed her head, and someone giggled. "This all started as a sort of a joke, a dare. The four of us have been getting each other into trouble since high school, and I can assure you we never thought it would go this far. We thought she would only get our four votes! But we were wrong, and it's a done deal now, so we have to figure out how this is going to work."

Johnny Ray stepped to the front. "Good afternoon, folks. I'm Johnny Ray Reynolds, and I was with these guys here when this whole thing got started. I'm going to read the swearing-in oath to Milly. If she turns away or tries to leave, we'll take that as refusal of the job, and the runner-up—you all know Mayor Linden—will be mayor, and we can swear him in. If she stays in place, we'll assume she accepts the job. We've even sort of stacked the hay in Arthur's favor, so when Dan lets go of the lead, she may be tempted to take a lunch break, and we'll swear in Arthur. That sound fair?"

Johnny Ray didn't know that Ralph had slipped back earlier and fed Milly. She wasn't hungry for any more hay at the moment. People were shrugging their shoulders and nodding their heads. Some thought it was funny, some thought it was a little surreal, but one person was clearly not ready to accept this plan. Arthur stood up. "Look, this can't be real. You can't run a mule for mayor. I was the leading candidate on the ballot, so I'm the mayor."

"Well, I don't know, Arthur," Steve spoke up. "I did some math, and you only got about 19 percent of the registered voters' support. That's hardly a mandate of the citizens. Milly only got 30 percent. So in reality, it's the city of Bridgeford who caused this circumstance. When less than half of the registered voters turn out to vote, and more than half of them don't even know anything about the candidate they vote for, well, I've heard it said you get the government you deserve."

With that, Johnny Ray started to read the oath to Milly. "Milly Harless, do you promise to uphold the laws of the city of Bridgeford and promote the welfare of its citizens? Do you further promise to devote your energies and abilities to the betterment of our community, protect our children, and represent us well to the surrounding communities? Will you respond to all concerns brought before you at City Hall meetings and advocate for initiatives that will enhance our town? If you are willing to take on the responsibilities of mayor of Bridgeford, please indicate by looking this audience right in the eye." Dan dropped Milly's lead. The crowd actually leaned forward to see if Milly would look away. Milly stood still as a statue. Stan was scribbling as fast as he could, and Alex was snapping photos of Milly with Johnny Ray's upheld right hand, the large brick City Hall clearly in the background.

"Congratulations, Ms. Mayor. We look forward to your leadership for the coming four years." Ralph was smiling from ear to ear as the gathered crowd started to applaud and cheer. The cheers sounded a lot like laughter.

Arthur hurried up to the stage. "Folks, I'm as surprised as you are by all this. I figured I was automatically going to win. I'll offer Milly my years of experience as mayor and my advice as assistant mayor. I can attend meetings when she's not able. That is, if it's OK with you, Milly." He looked at Dan and Ralph. They glanced at each other and shrugged their shoulders. "That sounds OK to me," Dan said.

"How will Milly conduct business?" Dan recognized Stan's voice.

"We actually thought about that this week while we were building this stage. I think we've come up with something that will work. We can present Milly with a question, and if she paws the ground once, it means 'No' and if she paws the ground twice, it means 'Yes,' and we'll proceed from there and see how it goes."

The man in the third row was Bobby Martin who owned the local locker plant. Being the town's butcher, almost everybody called him Butch. He stood up. "How are you going to know when it's a yes? What if she waits a long time for the second hoof to drop?"

"Well, I hadn't thought of that," Dan replied. "There will be a lot of things we'll have to figure out as we go along. But for this, maybe we set a time limit. If she hasn't pawed a second time within ten seconds of the first time, it's a no." Then just for a lark, he turned to Milly. "That sound OK to you?"

Milly had been standing still for a long time and was getting restless. She pawed the ground. Someone in the crowd started counting down "ten, nine, eight, seven..." The whole crowd took up the count. "Six, five, four..." Ralph nudged her a little. Milly shuffled her feet to shift her weight with three seconds to spare. Alex took a picture.

"Done!" Ralph shouted. "Now, folks, I know this is not what you were expecting, and I suppose you want to talk amongst yourself here for a bit. Jenny's got some coffee and sandwiches in the back, so sit down, have a bite to eat, and Milly's administrative managers"—he pointed to the three others on stage—"will be here to answer questions until one thirty. Official mayor hours will be from noon to two here at the bus station on Saturdays. Any business you want to bring to the attention of the mayor, we'll be meeting out back in the bus lanes. Now, if anybody in the crowd wants to come up and have your picture taken with Mayor Milly, come on up. Milly's very friendly and wants to meet you."

Dan led Milly down the ramp. Alex was taking more pictures. Stan was still scribbling as fast as he could.

10

Dan, Ralph, Steve, and Johnny Ray finished up morning chores early, and after a quick breakfast at Jenny's, they walked down the block to the back of the bus station. Stan's blue sedan could be seen at the curb, and as Milly was being led off the trailer, he and Alex came running up with notepad and camera at the ready.

"Hi, fellas," he greeted them.

"Hi, Stan," they replied.

"Hi, Alex. How's the newspaper business these days?" Steve asked.

Stan grinned. "Well, we knew there would be extra papers sold, so they printed a thousand extra copies. All sold out!"

"What?" Ralph looked surprised. "A thousand more than usual and you sold out?"

"Yep," Stan answered. "Evidently a Velka City TV newscaster said something about Milly, and the papers started selling."

"Well, how do you like that," Johnny Ray said. "She's only been mayor for eighteen days, and already business is picking up."

"What's on the Mayor's Meeting agenda today?" Stan asked.

Dan scratched his head. "Well, Milly doesn't really have an agenda. We'll just deal with issues that the community brings to her attention as they arise. We don't really expect a big turnout. Seems like apathy got her elected. Most likely folks have gone back to their regular ways."

At that moment, the first of the interested citizens of Bridgeford arrived. Arthur Linden was in the second group. By noon, about fifty people had gathered, and Dan called the meeting to order. "Folks, there's no chairs out here, so in the future, if you want, bring your lawn chairs. We aren't expecting this to take too long."

Arthur raised his hand. "I haven't removed my personal items from the office in the City Hall. I assume Milly won't be using that space. Is that right?"

Dan smiled. "No, I don't think she'll be needing that space. But I do hear that the City Hall is running out of space for the volunteers coordinator. Maybe they could use that suite now," he hesitated, and the pause gave extra weight to his next words, "since you're not actually the mayor after today."

Steve saw Arthur start to bristle and spoke up. "Milly doesn't want to rush you, Arthur. What do you say to vacating the space by the end of next month? That's about five weeks. We know you weren't expecting this."

Some were nodding their heads; some were trying hard to hide grins and not chuckle aloud. Arthur looked puzzled. "Well, I guess," he said.

Dan addressed the rest of the gathering. "Does anybody else have any business to bring before the mayor today?" he asked.

"What about the mayor's salary?" someone asked. "Are you guys going to get that money?"

Ralph looked at Dan, who shrugged, shook his head slightly. Ralph spoke, "Well, Milly doesn't need it, so if it's all right with everyone, I suggest it be donated to the Parks and Recreation budget. As one of Milly's administrative managers, I looked at the city's budget, and that seemed the most severely underfunded. Is everybody OK with that?"

He looked over at Dan and Steve and Johnny Ray, who were all grinning and nodding. The small group clapped and nodded—the city park in town did need some new wood chips, and the one by the river needed gravel in the parking lot. At the sound of the clapping, Milly stepped around a little, and someone pointed, "Look, she pawed twice. Mayor Milly approved."

"My daughter asked if we can have rides at the county fair this year," one lady asked. "She really liked the Ferris wheel last year at the state fair."

Steve stepped forward. "I was on the county fair committee last year, and I can tell you it's expensive to get a traveling carnival ride outfit to come because we're not on the route. But we can maybe hold some sort of fundraiser and try to get a few rides to come in. They usually want a deposit in advance, you know, in case of rain and poor turnout."

A man in the back had been silent but observing. Now he raised his hand. "Well, fellas, I own that big parcel of land you've been holding the fair on, and I'll waive my rental fee if you'll cover the insurance for the event."

Milly's administrative managers exchanged glances, and Ralph motioned to Steve to respond. "Ma'am, if you tell your daughter no promises, but Milly and her administrative managers will be working to maybe get a few rides at the fair this year. Milly is a city elected official, and the fair is a county event, but I think we can all work together to make it better for our citizens." Johnny Ray gave his friend a nod of approval for the great on-the-spot response. Steve was a natural leader.

"She'll be so happy. Maybe we can organize a bake sale to help. We can sell Milly's Macaroons." The rest of them laughed, and even Arthur had a grin on his face.

"Well, if there's no other business for the mayor this morning, I gotta get to the farm supply store before I head home," Ralph said.

"Meeting adjourned," Dan pronounced with a ring of authority he didn't usually feel.

The next week, Margaret Sanders, one of the Ditzy Dozen at Amanda's bridge party, spoke representing the Ladies Auxiliary of St. Cecelia's, making a request for a large creche to be placed on the lawn of City Hall.

"Very well," Steve said. "Milly, should we have religious symbols on the City Hall lawn as a permanent installation?" People waited. Milly didn't move. After a few moments, Milly pawed the ground in front of her once. The countdown began. "Ten, nine, eight..."

When they got to "one," Milly had looked around but hadn't moved her feet. Dan said, "Well, Milly says no, so I guess that's that. Is there any other business before the mayor today?"

Margaret was not pleased. Steve spoke up. "Margaret, we probably shouldn't have something from one church unless we have something from all the churches." Then he had an idea that might make her happy. "But maybe what we can do is repaint that big welcome sign out on the highway at the city limits that lists all the churches in town, and if you want a crèche painted on it by St. Cecelia's name, I don't see any problem with that. That sound OK to you?" Margaret nodded. Steve turned to Milly.

"Milly, what do you think of repainting the welcome sign at the edge of town?"

Johnny Ray was behind Milly, not drawing any attention to himself. He leaned into Milly's back hip, and she shifted away from him. "I saw her foot move twice," Margaret said. "Milly approved."

"Well, OK, then," Dan said. "We'll repaint the sign. Each church can paint a symbol of their choice on their section of the sign, and the city will provide the paint."

Jenny made enough money at her Sidewalk Café at mayor meetings that she had a big sign painted near the welcome sign on the highway, "Come on in to Bridgeford and see the town that has the first mayoral candidate to ever win with a write-in vote. Eat at Jenny's Café." At the café, the mayor's administrative managers sold copies of Milly's campaign poster for one dollar apiece to the travelers who stopped in. On the reverse side was a picture of Milly at the swearing-in and a brief story about the election.

Over the next several weeks, the gathering remained consistent at two to three dozen people. There were suggestions brought that Milly's administrative managers fielded, and some that Milly indicated her support or lack of support for, and always, there was Stan taking notes and Alex taking pictures. The *Velka City Sentinel* had started a weekly "Milly's Mayoral Minutes" column in the B section and listed the various city actions that had been approved or not.

11

The first Saturday in May was right before the high school graduation. Ralph started the Mayor's Meeting with an announcement. "Folks, next Saturday looks to be a pretty wonderful day in Bridgeford. Our high school seniors are going to be graduating, and you all know there will be a parade in honor of our proud graduates. Since Mayor Milly will be leading the parade, we'd like to declare it a town holiday and not hold mayor's office hours next week. Is that OK with everybody?"

The gathered citizens clapped and nodded. A chorus of "Good idea" and "I like that" and "My daughter's graduating" and other similar sentiments let Milly's managers know that the citizens attending thought the idea of a town holiday in honor of the graduates was a fine idea. "Is there any business to bring before the mayor today?" Ralph asked.

Sylvia Warner had come to the Mayor's Meeting with a determined step and a frown. She was carrying a plastic grocery sack that appeared to be full of some sort of paper. She had been followed shortly after by Ellie Villane, looking equally as stern. Sylvia reached the front and, standing straight as a soldier, spoke. "Dan, I have a complaint to make to the mayor."

Dan looked up, surprised. "Well, hello, Sylvia. You have a complaint about Milly? What's she done?"

"No, not about Milly. I have a complaint I want the mayor to address." She turned and looked pointedly at Ellie. "The complaint is about Ellie over there."

"OK, Sylvia. What's the problem?" Dan asked. He gave a quick glance to Steve and Johnny Ray, who were suddenly very busy looking at something else.

"Well, Dan," Sylvia began. "As you know, I own the Variety Emporium over on Second Street. I keep it clean and keep the sidewalk in front clean too. You know that, Dan," she said, perhaps a little more sternly than was necessary.

"Yes, Sylvia," Dan agreed, "I know you do. You keep a real nice place."

Sylvia cast another hard look at Ellie. "Well, on Friday nights, Ellie over there, she has her bingo games in the storefront next door. It's been vacant since the grocery moved out closer to the highway. Anyway, on Friday nights, she has a crowd come to her bingo games, and she sells hot dogs in those paper holders."

Ellie stood up. "I have all the permits I need, and I sell tasty hot dogs. Nothin' wrong with that. My hot dogs are good. Mustard and relish and chopped onion right there ready if you want them too." Sylvia was not the only person who could be emphatic.

"Now, Ellie, I know you do, I've had your hot dogs. They're right tasty," Dan soothed. He turned back to Sylvia. "What's the problem, Sylvia?"

Sylvia drew herself up as tall as she could. "Her customers *litter!* They litter the sidewalk with their little paper hot dog trays and wadded-up paper napkins. I come to open my store on Saturday mornings, and I have to pick up hot dog litter every week." With that, she opened the plastic bag she'd been holding and dumped out a torrent of little white paper hot dog trays on the pavement. "See what I have to deal with on Saturdays ever since she started selling hot dogs?"

Suddenly something seemed very funny to Steve and Johnny Ray, and they had their backs to the group. Ralph, who had the best poker face, stepped forward. "I have a solution to propose. If both of you agree to it, we can put it to Milly to officially endorse. Does that seem OK?"

"Well, let's hear it first," Sylvia pouted.

Ralph looked at Ellie. "Ellie, would you be willing to put an extra trash receptacle by the door so your bingo patrons can toss their trash away as they leave? Maybe with a sign that says, 'Help keep our town clean' or something like that?"

Ellie looked over at Sylvia. "I can do that."

Dan stepped forward. "And the mayor's office can put an outdoor trash can on the sidewalk between the two businesses to help those who step outside to finish their hot dogs."

"That's nice of you, Dan," Ellie said. She turned to Sylvia. "Honestly, Sylvia, if you had just said something to me, I would have cleaned it up. I lock up and leave by the back door, so I never noticed it."

"I didn't think of that," Sylvia said. "I always go out the front door when I leave the Emporium."

"OK, so I think we have a plan. Of course, it still needs the mayor's endorsement." Dan turned to Milly, and his voice took on an official ring. "Mayor Milly, we have an agreed plan between the two parties before you here today. Do you approve the placement of an extra trash receptacle on Second Street between the bingo hall and the variety store?" Milly stood there. Ralph bumped into her pretty hard, and it took her a few steps to maintain her place.

Everyone clapped, and Sylvia and Ellie shook hands. Ellie stooped down and started picking up the paper trays on the pavement in front of her. She looked up pointedly at Sylvia. "I'm willing to help, but I'm not willing to pick up everything you just dumped on the ground by myself."

"Oh, all right." Sylvia stooped to pick up some napkins and held the plastic bag open for Ellie.

"Next?" Dan called out to the group. When no one had anything else, Dan announced, "Meeting adjourned. So, let's all have some of Jenny's chicken salad sandwiches now."

12

The day of high school graduation dawned clear and warm. Knowing the parade would form at the large parking lot of the feed store and come down Oak to the city square, Jenny set up her Outdoor Café in the front yard of the bus station, where it had first served at Milly's swearing-in ceremony. Amanda greeted her as she set up her folding chair at the curb.

"Hi, Jenny," Amanda waved as she approached. "I'll take an iced tea."

"Hi, Amanda. Where are the girls? They're not old enough to be seniors yet, are they?" Jenny poured the iced tea and dropped in a wedge of lemon.

"No, they're sixth and middle school. But they wanted to watch the parade line up. John's with them." She sipped her tea.

"The Ditzy Dozen never anticipated all this, did they?" Jenny asked, amused.

"No, we sure didn't! But I bet it's been good for the café, and I think so far, it's been good for the town too."

"I think so too," Jenny said.

Amanda started to move off. "I'll get out of your way; you've got other customers here. See you Thursday evening."

Now the route around the City Hall Square was lined with people sitting on the curb or sitting in lawn chairs. Small children had little metal horns with flags that said "Congratulations Graduates" on them. John joined Amanda, and their two daughters were crowding to the curb to see better. They were tooting and waving with energy as Milly first came into sight, leading the parade toward them. Her administrative management team walked along, two on either side of her. Behind Milly, Arthur Linden's convertible glided along with the class king and queen, waving and smiling at the people on the sidewalk. Arthur was waving too. There were signs on either side of the car that read "Senior Royalty Ride sponsored by Mayor Emeritus Arthur Linden." Amanda looked across to catch Lucy's eye, and they grinned at each other. They each knew what the other was thinking: Arthur was still riding someone's coattails.

The senior float was next and had the remaining twenty-three graduates on a flatbed trailer decorated by the junior class with banners saying, "Seniors today, Leaders tomorrow" and "Bridgeford

Consolidated High School" on the sides. A pair of sheriff's deputies on motorcycles were making figure eights as they meandered after the senior float. There was a group from a children's dance class, pirouetting down the street. This was followed by the local martial arts trainees, in their official uniforms and belts indicating their level of proficiency. Both auto dealerships had a trio of bright, shiny new pickup trucks with banners proclaiming the name of the dealership. Then the town's bright-red ladder truck with eight volunteer firefighters in full gear clinging to the sides brought a round of applause as it passed by. The end of the parade was the high school band. Each year, the last performance of the band was the parade and graduation ceremony. While the graduation itself was solemn and dignified, each year the Marching Bears had a surprise song in the parade. A roar of cheers went up for the brass and woodwind rendition of Dolly Parton's famous "Muleskinner Blues." The parade lasted for eight blocks, and at the end of the route, there was a small celebration with cookies and ice cream from Jenny's Outdoor Café Two, staffed by the junior class.

13

The week after the graduation, folks gathering behind the bus station were opening lawn chairs and getting settled in when an unfamiliar car pulled up and parked. Two strangers emerged and headed for Stan and Alex of the *Sentinel*. Dan and Steve were watching and noticed that Stan had brought extra lawn chairs. Dan looked over at Steve and muttered under his breath, "This can't be good..."

"Let's go check it out," Steve replied.

They casually sauntered through the audience, nodding and saying hello to folks as they made their way to where Stan, Alex, and the two strangers were conferring. Stan saw them first and stood up. "Hi, guys. I want to introduce you to these two." He gestured toward the strangers, who stood. "These are Ben Terrace and John Schmidt from the television station KRMW in Velka. They've been following Milly in the *Sentinel* and wanted to come out and see for themselves. Your town's about to be famous." Dan and Steve offered their hands and gave their names.

Dan looked back at Stan. "I'm not sure the town particularly wants to be famous..."

"Dan, you have to admit, electing a mule as mayor is pretty unusual, and it's an interesting story," Ben said.

"Well, I suppose it is, and it's working out OK, but we don't need to be the laughingstock of the state," Steve said.

"We're not here to do that kind of a story," Ben said. "We actually think it's a great story, and there's no plan to make it sound ridiculous. We've been following some of the mayor's actions, and it seems like the town's doing quite well with Milly as mayor. It's a story of how the town started solving its problems by working together and helping each other. Lots of other towns could learn from this example."

Dan had his doubts. "Well, you fellas do what you have to, I guess. But remember, we're good, honest, hardworking folks here." He nodded, and he and Steve went back to the makeshift podium beside the horse trailer. Ralph had Milly out and standing to the side. A few children were petting her and talking to her.

Dan officially opened the mayor's office hours meeting and introduced the two newspeople from KRMW. Stan and Alex, having attended every meeting and stayed for chicken salad sandwiches and iced tea, had become almost like neighbors and no longer seemed like strangers to the local citizens.

"So," Dan continued, "is there any business to bring before the mayor's office this week?"

An elderly man raised his hand. Dan nodded at him in acknowledgment. He stood and introduced himself. "Mr. Harless, Mayor Milly, my name is Chester Browning, and I work at the City Hall in the office of the registrar of business licenses. I've worked there for over twenty-nine years. In fact, it will be thirty years on August first. I'm thinking I want to retire then. But I've got a problem, and I'm hoping the mayor can help me." He looked around, unsure whether to continue.

"Go on, Mr. Browning," Steve encouraged him. "I'm sure Mayor Milly will help if she can."

"Well, I can make it just fine on my Social Security after I retire. My place is paid for, and my needs are simple. But it's my grandson I'm worried about. I've been paying him out of my own pocket to do some odd jobs here and there. He got himself in a bit of trouble with the sheriff a while back, nothing serious, but he has to do community service for a while yet, and I know I won't be able to continue to pay him after I retire." He faltered again.

Dan nodded. "Yes, I remember when that happened, Chet. He's a good boy, just got in with kids who hadn't settled down yet. His name's Chet too, right?"

Chet looked up. "Well, actually it's Charles, but people called him Little Chet, after me, I guess. I had this idea." He hesitated, then continued. "The parks really need someone to be sort of a caretaker, and it would only be for one or two days a week, and with my salary not costing the city, maybe you could see your way to let him have that job maybe official-like. Give him some spending money, and some pride. His community service is about up, and he likes what he's been doing. He could do it for pay, like a real job. He'd really like a shirt with his name on the pocket. Do you think the city could do that? Maybe give him some confidence, maybe even some encouragement to take some classes at that community college—horticulture or something, maybe? He's a good boy but not very motivated. His folks got divorced three years ago and fight like cats and dogs. He pretty much stays at my place now, and I've been kind of looking after him since then. I worry about what will happen with him when I get old." He grinned a little. "Well, when I get older, anyway."

Ralph spoke for the first time. "Well, that's a nice idea, Chet, but what about your job? Who will do the work you've been doing after you retire? Wouldn't we need that money to pay them?"

"I thought of that, and as you may know, there are two of us in that office. I talked to Sharon, and she says what with the way we've computerized some of our processes, we're more efficient now than we were thirty years ago, and she is sure she can keep up with everything if she has just a part-time person to help her—maybe two or three days a week..." his voice trailed off.

Steve looked at his three friends. They nodded, and Steve stepped forward again. "I think we can agree to that. But just to be official, let's make an official proposal to Milly." He turned to the mule. "Milly, do you approve the splitting of Chet's job into two part-time jobs when he retires, one for the Parks Department and one to stay in Licenses?" Milly felt the nudge in her back flank and sidestepped toward Steve. Two steps. "Approved!" Dan shouted.

The gentlemen from KRMW were nodding and smiling.

Ralph stepped to the front. "Folks, if there's not any more business for the mayor, we've got a suggestion. The town is entitled to the full two hours of time the mayor agreed to be available. We noticed that the kids have enjoyed petting Milly and having their picture taken with her, and we're wondering if any would like a ride around the block on her back. I'll lead her slow and gentle-like for five dollars, and the money can go to the Rides at the Fair fund. Ride for Rides, we can call it." Children were clapping and turning to their parents for a five-dollar bill. Children too young to ride Milly alone sat in front of Ralph for free, with his strong arm around them to keep them safe.

14

It was now mid-May, and Saturday morning at Jenny's Café found the mayor's administrative managers at their usual table, eating breakfast and planning for the county fair. They had pulled up a table to adjoin theirs when they were joined by Sammy Baxter, the county commissioner and de facto point person for the fair, and Brian Douglass, the man who had waived the rental on his property as long as the event was properly insured. Ralph wiped his mouth and put his napkin in his empty plate. "Brian, we want to thank you again for the generous use of the fields behind your place for the county fair. I've talked to Jack down at United Insurance who has the policies for the county, and he assures me the county is covered for the event. It's written into the annual policy. So, there's no extra cost, the fair was budgeted for already."

"Even if there are rides, like a merry-go-round and Ferris wheel? We've never had them before, and if all this fundraising works, we might be able to have one or two rides," Sammy asked.

"That's a good point. I'll have to ask him if we need some kind of a rides rider for that." Ralph made a note in his pocket notebook, chuckling at his lame humor.

Jenny refilled coffee cups all around, and Brian was adding sugar to his cup. "How's that coming, anyway?" he asked.

"Steve had the flyers made. Since his last one was so successful," Ralph answered. They all looked at Steve, and he grinned and took another bite of his omelet. "Well, we looked into that, and it would cost us $2,000 per ride per day, so for three days, we would have to raise $6,000 for a 50 percent deposit. We're offering rides around the City Hall on Milly after the Mayor's Meeting on Saturdays. Five dollars a ride, all proceeds go to the rides fund. So far, we've got $480. But we're also going to use some of the money budgeted for the rental of your fields to make it up—that was $1,500, right, Sammy?" Sammy nodded, and Ralph continued. "We figured we could allot $1,200 of it for the rides. So now we need to raise an additional $4,320. We were thinking of using the other $300 of your budgeted rental to pay Chet's grandson and let him bring a friend to clean up the grounds while he's there—$50 a day each ought to get them pretty motivated. I'll tell them I'll make inspection rounds throughout the day to be sure the trash cans are kept emptied. That sound OK to you, Brian?"

"That sounds fine, guys. Anything I can do to help?"

"Well, if you can think of a different thing than rides on Milly, it might be good to have a different fundraiser," Johnny Ray spoke up. "We don't want to compete with the churches' summer bake sales, but we figure we've already got a five-dollar bill out of every kid who wants a ride, so that might be slowing down. We need something else to get us the rest of the money."

"You could have a decorated hat auction," Brian suggested. "Like they used to have in the old days. I remember my grandmother talking about that."

"How does that raise money?" Dan asked.

"Well, it's the ladies, mostly. They all go get themselves a plain straw hat. Then they decorate it with flowers, ribbons, little trinkets, make it fancy, and then the hats all get auctioned off. I know because I have a picture of my grandmother in the hat she made for an auction back when she was dating my grandpa," Brian explained. "She made this fancy hat with flowers and little birds and ribbons, and Grandpa bid on it to get her to pay attention to him. She wore it every anniversary of their marriage for fifty-three years. She was buried in it. He won that hat for a whopping seven dollars, which was a whole lot of money in those days. He used to say it was the best money he ever spent."

Steve spoke up. "We'll have to let Sylvia know to stock up on plain straw hats, but I think it could work. We haven't had anything like that in town that I can remember."

"We'll have to let people know somehow. We'll need to put up more posters," Johnny Ray said.

"Entrance fees will be one dollar to cover the cost of the notices, which we could place in all the windows that Milly's election posters were in. Each location could have entrance forms, and contestants can drop them off at Jenny's Café with their entrance fee any time before the fair."

"How would we pay for the rides with money we didn't have yet?" Ralph asked.

Johnny Ray spoke up. "My brother-in-law is vice president of the bank. I'm sure he would give us a short-term loan for a few weeks until the auction proceeds come in."

"Well, that's an issue for the next Mayor's Meeting, I guess," Dan replied. "We'd have to ask the town if they were willing to take a risk of a one-year tax hike to cover the difference. It wouldn't be more than one dollar apiece or so. They could pay it when they pay their county taxes."

"Or maybe some local businesses would sponsor the auction for $100, and we could put their names on the entrance forms," Ralph said. "That would help defray the cost, and it wouldn't have to get in the middle of tax assessments. I'm sure Randy at the grocery would go for it, and probably some others. Maybe Sylvia at the Variety Emporium, since she'll be making a nice little profit on the hats."

"We're taking a chance here, but if we can get the loan for no interest for a month and get the sponsorships and the proceeds of the auction, it just might work," Dan said. "This whole thing started out with no idea we'd be doing this, but so far, we've managed to do some good things for this town. Let's take a chance and do this."

That afternoon at the Mayor's Meeting behind the bus station, the mayor's administrative managers shared the idea of the hat auction, and those in attendance nodded and clapped at the idea. Joan Barton was there, and she raised her hand when the chatter subsided.

"Yes, Joan? You have something for the mayor?"

"I do, Dan," she answered, rising from her chair. "I think it would be a great idea if some of the local businesses supported the Hat Auction even if they weren't official sponsors. I know my bakery would like to participate, but I don't know if I can afford a full sponsorship, and I want to ask Milly if she likes the idea of Milly's Muffins, from now until the end of the summer fair, and I'd donate fifty cents from every muffin for the rides fund."

"Well, that sounds pretty wonderful, Joan," Dan smiled at her. "What kind of muffins would they be?"

"You know everybody likes my pineapple and coconut muffins. I've been calling them Piña Colada Muffins. But if Milly approves, I'll call them Milly's Muffins until the end of the fair."

Dan looked over at Milly, who was looking kind of bored. "Joan, Milly already approved a fund for the rides. I don't think we need to approve every separate initiative that goes into that fund. People have sometimes just been making donations." He looked over to Steve and Johnny Ray, who nodded. He glanced over at Ralph behind Milly, ready to lose his balance and fall against Milly if needed. He nodded too. Dan continued, "I think you're welcome to do that, and we'll be glad to help spread the word. Maybe flat-out $250 is for sponsors, and the individual initiatives like Milly's

Muffins could be listed as supporters on the flyer, so people would know to support them."

Jerry Perkins was the only Realtor in Bridgeford, and he also did some maintenance at City Hall. He stood to speak. "Yes, Jerry," Dan acknowledged.

"Dan, you know I own that building that used to be a grocery store, where Ellie has her bingo on Friday nights. It's vacant the other days of the week, but there's a lot of people on that street. Seems to me that you're going to wind up spending a lot of time putting out flyers all over town, and people might run out of room for them. I'd like to offer the storefront window for information about the mayor's activities, and we could have a fundraising section with just one poster that would be right in that big front picture window. And I'd be happy to put a framed bulletin board just inside the entrance to City Hall, and people could see them there. Maybe just have two main focal points, unless you'd rather be making a whole bunch of posters. I think people are going to get behind this so the kids can have a merry-go-round at the fair. Maybe even a Ferris wheel."

Dan and the others had been nodding as he spoke. "I appreciate that, Jerry," he said. "I can make a notice that if someone has a money-making event, they can drop off two posters at Jenny's and I'll pick them up on Saturday mornings, see that you get them that same day."

Burt Moseley owned Moseley's Grocery, the grocery store that had moved out closer to the highway. He raised his hand. "I have something to offer. I don't know if you want a poster for it or not," he said.

Dan nodded for him to continue.

"The baggers at the store are mostly all high school kids, especially on Saturdays when so many folks get their groceries, and the older baggers want the weekend off. They've all volunteered to donate all their tips between now and the fair to support getting a Ferris wheel. I'll make you up a sign for that if you think it could go in Jerry's storefront with the hat auction and muffins. And the courthouse, too, of course. We could even put out a tip can for both the Ferris wheel and the merry-go-round. We'll let the customers vote which one is closer to the front gate. The one with the most donations wins. I even thought of a slogan—*Baggers CAN be choosers!* What do you think?"

"That's really generous of them, Burt. Don't they want to hang on to some of it for movies and such?" Steve asked.

"Oh, I guess they'll just use their regular paycheck for that. They're just talking about the tips from shoppers when they carry the bags and load them into the cars."

"Sounds good! Tell them we appreciate it, and Milly appreciates the young folks supporting a municipal fund drive like this," Steve said.

"How about a little friendly competition, Burt?" Randy asked. "Food-Rite can do the same thing, and we'll combine the monies at the end, but the store that raises the most money gets bragging rights and a sign or something."

"I like that, Randy. Moseley's will be glad to have you join us in that."

When no one else stood up to speak, Dan adjourned the meeting.

15

The Sunday morning edition of the *Velka City Sentinel* featured an article with Stan's byline. Wrapped around a picture of Milly giving a small child a ride, with City Hall clearly in the background, it had earned a spot on the editorial page.

Bridgeford Citizens Get Involved

We've been reporting for a few weeks now on the aftermath of the town of Bridgeford electing a mule, Milly Harless, to the office of mayor. It started as a joke between friends, and up to now, it's all been pretty much in fun. But at yesterday's Mayor's Meeting, an interesting phenomenon occurred. A few weeks ago, at Milly's swearing-in ceremony, one of the citizens said her daughter wished Milly could get the county fair to have rides like a merry-go-round or a Ferris wheel. This week, the town responded with a resounding, "We'll sure try!"

Milly has been offering rides for kids after the weekly Saturday Mayor's Meeting, and now other fundraising efforts of the locals are taking shape. There will be an auction of straw hats decorated by local citizens. The local bakery is offering muffins renamed Milly's Muffins, with a portion of the proceeds from the sales going to the cause. The town's youth are getting into the act as well. The grocery sackers at the town's two local markets are donating all their tips to the fund! Perhaps they have visions of being at the top of the Ferris wheel with their date.

In any case, we can't help but notice that in a town of only 2,442 people, the past decade or so has seen very little that brings them together in a common cause, and since Milly was elected, they've managed to create at least one new job, get more trash receptacles on the sidewalks, refresh the town's welcome sign, get the rental fee for the use of the fairgrounds waived, and start a drive to get rides at the fair. Mules may have a reputation for being stubborn, but the citizens of Bridgeford are getting a reputation for being actively involved in their town's future. It all started as a joke among four old friends where a mule got elected through a combination of voter apathy and voter ignorance or misguided reasons, but now it has turned the town into a model of camaraderie and unity and activity among the citizens of all ages that is solving problems and bringing improvements to the town.

This is doubly ironic, given that Milly's election was a direct result of most people in the town *not* being actively involved in its politics. For those who haven't been following this column, Milly was elected as a write-in candidate. Her name was not on the ballot at all. And other than the four friends who started the Milly for Mayor Campaign on a dare, as a joke, no one who wrote in Milly's name knew who she was. Or that she was a mule. Some just wanted change—any change. Some simply wanted a female. Some were supporting friends who were supporting Milly. But it's clear, nobody knew Milly was a mule, nobody thought a mule would actually be elected. The previous mayor had served the town well. No hint of scandal or abuse. He'd been reelected two times before. People simply voted for someone else. Blindly.

Perhaps embarrassed by the result of their action, perhaps out of curiosity, they've become more involved in their town's concerns. They've started to fix their problems. The parks have new bark on the playground. The town is cleaner. People are attending City Hall citizen meetings. These citizens have been more active in the town's concerns in the last two months than they have in the last 10 years. Perhaps electing Milly was the right thing to do. Perhaps other towns need to have a mayor like Milly.

That night at six thirty, Ralph was just putting away the supper dishes when his phone rang. He didn't usually get calls on Sunday nights from anyone, and there was a little tightening of the nerves as he picked up the receiver. Dan's voice came on, sounding alarmed. "Ralph. Turn on your TV right now. KRMW."

"What's up?" Ralph was picking up the remote control as he spoke.

"Just do it!" Dan insisted, not sounding happy at all.

Teddy Thompson, the evening news anchor, was talking to the camera and the coanchor. "We've heard of a place going to the dogs, Christie, but this is the first time I've ever heard of a place going to the mules. Last April, the small farming community of Bridgeford elected a mule to the office of mayor, and now the mule, whose name is Milly, is running the town."

Christie took up the story. "This may be the first time a write-in candidate has ever won an election, at least in this state. And apparently, only four people in the small town knew she was a mule. We sent a news team down to investigate. Ben, what did you learn?"

A video insert appeared to the right of the anchor desk, and Ben Terrace in Dockers and a polo shirt was smiling directly into the camera. In the background, a small group of children were petting Milly while Ralph held her halter. "Well, Christie, apparently last January, four longtime friends dared each other it couldn't be done, and on a bet, made up some flyers to elect Milly Harless as a write-in candidate. Word spread, and enough people did it, not as a joke, that Milly ousted the incumbent Arthur Linden by 24 percent."

The camera shifted to a close-up of Milly, with Ralph helping a child up on Milly's back. Ben's voice continued over the video. "Milly has been giving rides to raise money for a Ferris wheel at the county fair this year, and some of the town's residents have invented their own fundraising ideas to support that. Jenny Rendon, owner of Jenny's Café, where this all started, tells us that the citizens are more involved in this initiative than they have been for anything in years. Milly has approved a new part-time job without raising payroll costs and approved extra trash cans on the sidewalks to help reduce litter."

Christie spoke as the camera followed Milly clopping out of sight behind the City Hall, "Sounds like a story we'll be following for a while, Ben. Thanks for checking this out for us." The video went blank, and the screen recentered on the two in the newsroom.

Teddy smiled into the camera. "Well, Christie, with all that fundraising and such, they may be going to the mules, but they're sure not going to the dogs!"

"They're certainly not, Teddy. They're like the little town that could. I do have to wonder, though, is it even possible to elect a mule as mayor? Is it legal?"

Dan and Ralph had both been gripping their phones but not speaking. But when they heard her question the legality, they both groaned. "I was afraid this could get us in trouble," Dan said.

"Shhhhhh, wait 'til they're done," Ralph said under his breath.

Teddy was answering Christie's question. "I'm not sure, Christie. There's probably more to come on this story. But next, we have an update on the morning drive tomorrow. Sealia Drive will be closed for construction..."

Ralph and Dan both turned off their TVs at the same time. "Now what do we do?" Dan asked Ralph.

"We don't do anything. It's not illegal to write in a candidate's name. Nobody did anything illegal. It's working. The story was positive about the town, and this morning's paper was positive."

"This won't be the end of it. You know that, don't you?" Dan insisted.

"Yeah, probably not, but it's fun now, and it's not over yet," Ralph said. But then, as an afterthought, "Maybe you should ask your young nephew what could happen."

"I think I'll do that. He can look up legal stuff at the university or ask one of his teachers."

"OK, so we have a plan. Quit worrying for now. Just let the rest of us know what he says."

"I will, I will. You know if we all four wind up in jail over this, Milly isn't going to pardon us. You know that, don't you?"

"Good night, Dan." Dan could hear Ralph chuckling as he hung up the phone.

The next day, Dan called his nephew Jason and left a message that Jason should call back as soon as he could. Dan's wife was just putting the supper dishes in the sink when the phone rang. Dan picked up the receiver. "Hello?"

"Hey, Uncle Dan. This is Jason. I got your message. What's up?" Jason's voice sounded alarmed.

"We have a little issue down here in Bridgeford, son, and I thought since you helped get us into this mess..."

"What mess?" Jason asked.

"You got Ralph and Steve and Johnny Ray all excited about making Milly a write-in candidate. Now she's won, and things were kind of going along quiet-like, but today, it was on the TV news, and the news guy asked if it was legal. Ralph thinks it's funny, but I'm worried. Can we get in any trouble here? It was just supposed to be a joke."

"Well," Jason answered carefully. His uncle Dan and aunt Anna had taken him in when his parents were killed in that highway accident, and now he wanted to be sure his surrogate parents were OK. "I saw that guy on TV and figured you might be calling, so I did a little research."

"What did you learn, son? Are we in any trouble?"

"No, I don't think so. There's nothing illegal about anybody writing in a candidate of their choice, so nobody's in any trouble. What will probably happen..."

"Oh, Jason. I'm really glad to hear that," Dan interrupted. "What do you think will come of it—that TV news guy might get some people who don't even live here to try to make a fuss..."

"That's what I was trying to tell you, Uncle Dan. Nobody can get anybody into trouble. What can, and probably will, happen is that sooner or later some official will realize that a mule can't be mayor. They will use the reasoning that the write-in candidate never filed an affidavit with the county election board."

"What does that mean?" Dan asked, sounding a bit calmer.

"Well, when someone writes in a candidate, they usually only get four or five votes, nothing anywhere near any of the names that are officially on the ballot. So basically, nobody cares, and nobody does anything about anything. It's a nonissue. But technically, if someone knows they're going to be a write-in candidate, they file an affidavit with the election commission stating that they are a resident and a registered voter, and they're eligible to be elected. If they do get a significant number of votes, someone in the election commission office checks to be sure they filed an affidavit that states they are aware they are being suggested through write-in process and are legally eligible to be elected."

"What do you have to do to be legally eligible to be elected?" Dan asked.

"Most usually, it means you have to be a registered voter in the district that you've been written in for. In this case, Milly would have to be a registered voter in Bridgeford to be eligible to win."

"So why wasn't she disqualified on election night?" Dan asked.

"Well, probably because nobody complained," Jason replied.

"You may be right about that. The only one who was upset was Arthur, and he probably didn't want to publicize the fact that he'd been outvoted for a mule."

"Now you're getting it, Uncle Dan. If nobody in the town started a formal complaint, then probably nobody officially looked for an affidavit of eligibility on Milly. Everybody sort of just probably forgot to think about that part."

"But the news guy on TV just asked his coanchor if it was legal. Won't that start something?"

"I guess it could," Jason answered. "But the worst that can happen is Milly is disqualified, and Arthur is mayor again. It's really no big deal."

Dan interrupted. "Well, we're doing just fine with Milly, actually. Arthur's not upset, we're working on getting rides for the county fair, we just want to be left alone. Nobody's hurting anything."

"I know, I know. I think you should just not worry about it until someone complains. You can deal with it then."

"OK, but please, son, will you keep yourself tuned in with all this, and let us know if we need to do anything?"

"Sure, Uncle Dan. I've been following the little news items in the *Velka City Sentinel*. Milly and the town are doing good things. I wouldn't worry about what some newscaster said. He didn't talk about filing a complaint; he was just filling time on air."

"He just asked if it was even legal, and the other lady said she didn't know, then he started talking about road construction and the morning drive."

"So you're fine. Just don't do anything to make someone want to get involved."

"I'll tell the rest of the boys at breakfast tomorrow."

"I thought you guys ate breakfast every Saturday?" Jason asked.

"We do, but we're going to the bank tomorrow to ask for a line of credit for the deposit on the rides. I'll tell them then."

"I really think nothing will come of it, Uncle Dan," Jason replied.

"Thanks for calling back, Jason. Other than having a nervous uncle, how's the rest of school and life up there in the big city?"

They chatted a bit longer, and when they said goodbye, Dan was ready to tell the rest of Milly's administrative management team that none of them would wind up in jail over all this. He gave Anna a hug and started drying the dishes. "That Jason is a mighty fine boy, isn't he, Anna?"

"He sure is," she agreed and handed him another plate to dry.

16

On Monday, the administrative management team met at Jenny's Café to plan their approach to the bank. Dan was the first to speak after the coffee cups had been filled. "I talked to Jason yesterday, and he says we're not in any trouble." He gave a recap of Jason's assurances and continued, "I'm more relaxed now, but I still think this will all fall apart at some point."

"Yeah, maybe, but it's fun now," Ralph replied. "We've actually done worse stuff before."

Dan looked at the three of them. "Maybe so, but I just wanted you guys to know what Jason said. We're really here to talk about the line of credit at the bank, and it opens in forty-five minutes."

"I have a loan for my new tractor with Paul Fuller at First Security Bank. You guys know him, I think. He coached baseball for a while and has been with the bank for years."

"That's my brother-in-law," Johnny Ray spoke up. "I have a loan there too, for my new truck."

"He coached my sons," Ralph said. "I bank there too. That would be a good first place to ask."

Johnny Ray and Steve nodded. They compared notes on the cost, what they had so far, and the ideas they had to raise the rest. The four stood, swigged the last of their coffee, and left money on the table for Jenny and the tab.

First Security Bank had been one of the first buildings erected when Bridgeford was formed, and though it had kept up with all the technological changes throughout the years, it still had the look and feel of its original days. This made the ATM and security cameras seem oddly out of place.

"Hi, Betty," Dan said as they approached the receptionist desk. "We'd like to see Paul for a few minutes, if he's free."

"I think he is, but let me just check," she replied. She slid out of her chair and smoothed her skirt as she stood. "You boys wait here for just a minute." With that, she disappeared down a hallway. Within three minutes, she was back. "You can go right in. He's in the first office on the left."

"Thanks, Betty," Ralph said. He picked up a wrapped butterscotch candy from the small plastic bowl on her desk. "You know you shouldn't be offering these so early in the morning." He winked as he slipped it into his pocket.

"You know you shouldn't be taking them this early in the morning," she replied. It was clear this was an ongoing dialogue between the two.

When they got to Paul's office, he was just rolling in an extra chair from the next office. "Betty said there were four of you, so I had to grab a few extra seats. Hi, Ralph, Dan. Good to see you. Johnny Ray, Steve, good to see you too. Have a seat, let's see what's on your minds."

They all settled into chairs, and Ralph was the first to speak. "Paul, you probably know that the four of us here are the administrative managers for Mayor Milly." He said it with a straight face, and Paul, to his credit, nodded his head without any indication that there was anything unusual in this. Ralph continued speaking. "The mayor was asked to get rides here for the county fair, and we've been working on that. You've probably seen the posters in Burt's storefront on Second Street for the fancy hat auction and such. Well, we got confirmation from Midwest Midways and Carnivals that they're available for our fair dates. It's not that far off their regular route. The cost will be $2,000 per day per ride, so that's $12,000. But they need a deposit of 50 percent up-front and a guarantee of the full amount by the end of the contract, in case it's rained out and ticket sales don't materialize."

"Yes, I've seen the fundraising posters. The town is really getting behind this," Paul said.

Dan fished a sheaf of papers out of his jacket pocket. "I've got the contract right here. It says they get all proceeds of ride ticket sales until the full $12,000 is secured, and they split the rest with us fifty-fifty. If there are enough riders, we could make back our deposit and maybe even make some money. We're not too worried about it."

"So you want a line of credit for $6,000?" Paul asked.

"Well, not that much," Ralph picked up the conversation. "We've got $1,680 so far from what we've done, and we expect the fancy hat auction to be pretty successful, and the baggers have committed all their tips, but it would be probably pretty close to $4,000 at least until the end of the fair when we see how much the sale of ride tickets made."

Johnny Ray spoke up. "We're hoping that you can spot us a short-term, low-interest line of credit on our signatures. You know us all, we've been here all our lives. Heck, you were best man at my wedding. And if we wind up short after the fair, we'll continue to have more fundraisers. I'm sure the folks of the town will back us, but we can't send in the contract until we know we can meet their conditions."

Paul smiled. "I don't see a problem with that at all. If you'll trust a handshake now, I'll have Betty draw up the documents and you can sign them Monday or Tuesday. In the meantime, what account do you want to send them the check from?"

Ralph said, "Well, I've been holding on to the cash we've got so far at the house, but it should probably be in the bank. I can bring it by Monday."

"Great," Paul said. "I'll open an account for you this afternoon and put the line of credit on it. You can use a bank draft today for $6,000 to go with your contract and pick up checks and deposit slips Monday." He stood and held out his hand, and all four rose with him and shook his hand in turn, thanking him. "You know," Paul said more conspiratorially, "I voted for Milly. I don't know why, but it seemed like it was time to do something different."

They stopped at Betty's desk on the way out. Paul gave her the overview of the plan, and she drew up a check and handed it to Ralph. "See you Monday, Betty," Ralph winked. "Be sure that bowl is here."

"When has it ever not been?" she snorted. But she winked back.

That evening, Ralph and his wife were just sitting down to supper. The television in the front room was tuned to WGN in Chicago. Even though the volume was low, they both heard the announcer say, "And for our feel-good closer tonight, we have news from our Velka City station. They do things a bit differently in those parts. The citizens of Bridgeford have elected a mule as their mayor in the most recent election. And we don't mean a stubborn person, we mean a real mule. And evidently, the citizens didn't realize Milly was a mule but voted for her as a write-in candidate, based on flyers distributed around town on a dare. Well, we know who won: The city won because they've already upgraded some city infrastructure, refreshed the ground cover at a city park, and now they're raising funds to get rides for the county fair. If that doesn't make you feel good, we can't help you. Good night, folks."

Ralph sighed. Louise picked up his plate and put it in the oven to stay warm. "Why you doin' that?" he asked.

"You know Dan's gonna be on the phone before you can finish dinner." Ralph nodded resignedly. The phone rang.

"Hi, Dan," Ralph said.

"Ralph, I was listening to the news out of Chicago this evening, and we're a national story! Not a big one, but a national station is talking about us. Somebody's gonna send somebody to make us get Milly out of the mayor's office."

"Is that what the news story said?" Ralph asked.

"No, at least not yet. But you know it's gonna happen," Dan grumbled.

"Well, maybe," Ralph agreed. "But they haven't yet, so let's just see what happens. We never thought she'd get in office in the first place, remember?"

"You know we can't keep this up forever, don't you? You know a mule can't really be mayor, don't you?" Dan was pleading his usual refrain.

Ralph smiled and countered with, "Don't worry, Dan. It will all be fine. Remember what Jason said."

"I know, I know, but this is getting bigger and bigger. WGN is Chicago," Dan replied.

"I know. It was just a feel-good closer. Nobody pays attention to those," Ralph replied. "I gotta go. Louise is holding my dinner, so I'm going to hang up now. I'll see you Saturday at Jenny's." With that, he hung up the phone.

17

Betty and SueEllen approached the counter at Sylvia's Emporium to pay for their purchases. Sylvia began to ring up Betty's items, and as she rang up the plain straw hat, she said, "Betty, this is the first hat out of the third order I've had to make. There were two dozen in each of the previous orders, so that means at least forty-nine hats will be auctioned off."

SueEllen spoke up. "You mean fifty hats. I have one here too."

"Yes, SueEllen," Sylvia continued, "yours would make fifty. I'm really eager to see what they look like. People have been buying ribbon and artificial flowers, and all kinds of other things. One even bought cookie cutters to put on hers."

Betty paid for her purchases and waited while SueEllen put her items on the counter. "I plan to do something a bit different, and I'm not telling what!"

"That sounds wonderful, Betty," Sylvia answered. "I'm sure it will be lovely."

SueEllen said, "Well, if you're going to keep it a secret, you won't be working on it at Ditzy Dozen night?"

"Oh," Betty replied. "I hadn't thought of that."

Sylvia saw the dilemma and quickly said, "Well, you could get the other eleven to swear to secrecy, I bet."

"Yes," SueEllen exclaimed. "That's it. We'll all swear not to tell anyone what any of us at Amanda's is making."

"Thanks, Sylvia," Betty said, giving her a quick hug. "See you soon."

The following Thursday night, the Ditzy Dozen met at Amanda's home. All the card tables were set up, but no cards were in sight. Instead, they were all working with glue guns, needles and thread, and a variety of ribbons, bows, miniature plastic birds and bees, and other ornamentation. Some had huge Victorian brims, ties that made big bows under the chin. Some were more prim. Some had large plumes that swayed in the air above the hats.

During a lull in the conversation about the hats, Amanda raised her voice so everyone at the tables could hear her. "Ladies, I have an announcement. Or maybe it's more of a question. Yesterday, a man came into the shop and said he was from the secretary of state's office. He wanted to know what we knew about the election of the mule. I wasn't rude, but it sounded like he was looking to make us get rid of Milly. I told him I didn't know where she lived. I suggested the best thing would be to come to a Mayor's Meeting on Saturday, and I called Ralph to let him know. Do you think this guy can cause us any trouble?"

"I don't know," Margaret said. "I guess in the long run, a mule probably can't be mayor. But it's working for us, and those city folks should just leave us alone."

"I know," Lucy said. "As long as Arthur was the runner-up, and actually he's doing more now than he did before, I don't see any reason to change anything."

"Well, if they try to make us do something, we can tell them Arthur is mayor and just keep doing what we're doing now," SueEllen said.

There were vigorous head nods and murmurs of agreement. It was clear these ladies weren't going to let some bureaucrat from out of town come and tell them what to do. Polly added another sliver of silver paint to the felt hatband she was decorating. This particular streak of silver was part of a fireworks display over the familiar silhouette of the Bridgeford City Hall building. The strip of felt also had miniature depictions of Milly, the welcome sign at the city limits that had been freshly painted, and the outline of a Ferris wheel, all nestled into the letters spelling out Bridgeford and the year.

18

The mayor's administrative management team was having their usual Saturday breakfast at their usual table in the back of Jenny's Cafe. They didn't notice the man at the next table with his back to them. He was dressed in jeans, a western-style plaid shirt, and brown cowboy boots. He did not look at all like he was an investigator for the election commissioner's office. But if the mayor's administrative management team had paid closer attention, they would have noticed that he didn't look like those clothes were his normal Saturday morning fare. The jeans were a bit too new and crisp, and the shirt looked starched. Had they paid him any attention, it would have looked like he was simply having coffee and reading the newspaper. Ralph handed out a single page to each of the others. "I wrote up a simple little report to let you guys know where we are on the money and the bank, and I gave a copy to Jack Barrows at United Insurance and Sammy Baxter at the courthouse so they're up to speed on everything. Between sponsors and supporters, we have deposited almost

$3,200 into our account at First Security. We only owe $1,845 on our line of credit. I asked Sylvia how many hats she'd sold, and she's almost through her third box of two dozen. So that's nearly seventy-two hats. If they all auction for $15, that would be another $1,080, and I'll bet some go for $20 or $25. I know of a couple ladies that have some competition for their hats. And Milly's Muffins have brought in another $105. If it rains the whole weekend, we'll need to pay Midwest Midways and Carnivals another $6,000 at the end of the fair, but weather will likely be good, and they keep all ticket sales until that's made. At $3 a ticket, that's only two thousand rides, between the Ferris wheel and the merry-go-round together. Plus, we have the tips and betting jar from the grocery store, so I'm sure we'll make our goal."

Steve chimed in. "You know, it didn't take nearly $72 to print those Auction Hat entrance forms, so we'll come out ahead on the $1 entrance fees from that, too."

After the conversation moved on to the weather, the upcoming grandchildren's birthdays, and such, the four friends didn't notice the man at the next table fold the newspaper and slip a small, hand-held tape recorder into his pocket. He paid for his coffee, gave an unremarkable tip, and left.

19

It was Wednesday just after noon when the caravan from Midwest Midways and Carnivals rolled into Bridgeford. They'd called Ralph when they were an hour out of town and let him know they were arriving soon. The gates to the large, flat fairgrounds were open, and though the local booths and animals and contestants for local competitions didn't arrive until tomorrow, the representative had said the crew liked to arrive and have their areas set out before the locals were setting up, as their rides were large and on multiple vehicles, so they wanted as much access as they could get to unload and set up.

Ralph, Dan, Steve, and Johnny Ray greeted Brian Douglass when he arrived and removed the padlock from the chain that bound the wide, swinging gates closed. "Thanks for meeting us out here, Brian. I could have picked up the key this morning," Steve said.

"Oh, no problem, buddy," Brian replied. "You boys know I'm happy to provide the space in this field, but I did sort of want to see the size of the trucks they'd be on and sort of watch to see if they dig big ruts in the field. And to tell you the truth, I really wanted to see a big Ferris wheel come rolling into town." He grinned.

Johnny Ray and Dan each walked one of the wide gates open until it was folded completely back against the fence. "It looks like I might not have been the only one." Brian pointed across the street, and there was a pack of a dozen or so adolescent boys in jeans and T-shirts trying to look nonchalant. "They keep looking down the highway like they know the rides are almost here."

"I'm betting somebody at the grocery on the highway saw them go past," Johnny Ray replied. "It doesn't take much to get word out on some things."

Just then the pack of youngsters started jumping and pointing, and some were crossing the street to the fairground entrance. "Now you boys keep back out of the way and off the highway," Johnny Ray said. "You can line up here inside if you stay close to the fence and don't get in the way."

Just as the last youngster had come in and joined his friends along the fence line, the first big truck appeared and slowed down, started its blinker, and turned in where Brian and Steve were waving the driver through the open gates. The driver was a big man with a straw cowboy hat pushed back on his head. He leaned out the window and grinned a toothless grin. "Mornin', gentlemen. Is one of you Ralph Wightman?"

Ralph stepped forward. "That'd be me. Welcome to Bridgeford."

"Thanks, glad to be here. I'm Ellis Whitson. I'm crew chief for this gig, and I'll be your primary contact if you have any questions or issues. You got a preference where we set up?"

"This whole field back here," Ralph waved his hand to indicate the field Brian was providing. "This whole field is usually just parking, but it's never full of vehicles. We figured the rides could be as close to the grandstand over there as is reasonable. The Ferris wheel won the penny vote on which would be closest to the entrance, so if you could set it up closest to these gates and the merry-go-round on the other side of the grandstand so people go past all the booths under the grandstand to ride both rides. We'll just have the parking guides start the first row of parking farther back."

"Sounds good to me. We've got some portable fencing we can put up to cordon off the rides from the parking. It's a safety thing, you know. We'll get the rides unloaded and the bases stabilized and move the trucks to that back edge of the field out of the way today, and we'll have most of the assembly done by dark. Then tomorrow we'll take care of the barrier fences by dawn, then the connections and safety checks and such. Fair opens Friday, right? The official safety inspector is scheduled for noon tomorrow."

"Yep, and tomorrow there will be others setting up for contests like jams and jellies and quilts and pies, and the 4-H will be bringing in their animals, but it doesn't open to the general public until Friday at eight o'clock in the morning."

"Think those boys over there would like to help unload? We got lots of 'go-fer' chores we could pay them to help, if they can take instruction and pay attention."

"Sure, they're all good boys, I know 'em all. My wife has had all of them in her class." With that, he turned and gave a sharp, loud two-finger whistle. "Boys, get over here." He turned back to the driver. "Best to pay them as a pack, keep them on the same team."

"How about if we give each of them ten tickets for free rides to help for an hour or so?"

"Now that's a great idea."

The rest of the trucks had pulled in, and a collection of both scrawny and burly men were gathering a bit removed from where these introductions had taken place. Ellis climbed down and conferred with them, pointing and waving his hands to let them know the setup plans. After a few moments, he returned to Dan, Ralph, and the rest of the Bridgeford men. Steve spoke first. "You guys know where the two motels are? You drove right past them as you came into town."

"Oh, we have camper trucks and are pretty self-contained. We need to stay close to the rides for safety purposes." Ellis held out his hand. "We're fine. Good to meet you all." They shook hands all around, and the men were already back in their trucks, telling the boys to "wave us into position, let us know when we're even with this edge here."

Ralph chuckled. "You know, if they can get those things here from northeast Texas, they can park them in an open field. They're just giving the boys some excitement."

Steve nodded. "And the boys will brag to their friends and chatter about it over dinner nonstop, and parents will want these guys back next year."

Dan smiled. "Nothing wrong with that."

Thursday, there was general activity in the grandstand booths as people set up various games of chance that were homemade and had been freshly repainted in anticipation of the rides and the first fair with Milly as mayor. Arthur Linden was on hand to assist and speak for the mayor's office since Milly wasn't coming into Bridgeford until Friday morning. He bustled about, giving unneeded instruction and sounding pretty official for someone who had lost the election, but everyone knew Arthur and no one was bothered.

The state inspector arrived right at noon, and by two o'clock the rides had been officially certified as safe for public operation.

20

Friday morning, the sun had barely risen and the men from Midwest Midways and Carnivals were already at their rides, checking that there had been no overnight mischief. Brightly painted food trucks were parked along the perimeter, and the proprietors were raising the awnings on the sides of the large vehicles, setting out pots of flowers and attaching the streamers and flags to catch the eyes of passers-by. The smell of bacon frying and fresh brewed coffee drifted through the air. The cooks greeted early vendors and a few early families. By eight thirty, people were arriving and greeting each other at the gate, children eager to run ahead and see the rides.

The first dozen people in line for the Ferris wheel watched eagerly as the ride operator inched the wheel forward enough to carefully put one car exactly at the loading platform. "Next two or three," he called out. Sylvia and her two grandchildren, Tina and Ryan, climbed on board. The operator closed the door and latched it securely. The wheel began to rotate but stopped just a few seconds later, the carriage swinging gently back and forth in place. Sylvia looked a bit alarmed, but her grandchildren were excited.

"Look, Gramma Syl," they cried. "That's Tracy and Jim from fourth grade getting on now." Sylvia realized the ride would only go a short bit around its path until all the cars were full, then it would begin to make its full circles. She relaxed and looked out across the grounds. "Gramma Syl, I bet we can see all the way to Velka City when we get to the top," Tina exclaimed. Soon every carriage was occupied, and the ride operator hollered out, "Everybody ready to ride the Ferris wheel?" A chorus of voices rang out, and the wheel began to rotate slowly.

On the opposite side of the fairgrounds, the same excitement was growing at the merry-go-round. Children were spotting the animal they wanted to ride, claiming "dibs" on the brightly painted wooden tigers, the elephants, the horses, and the giraffes.

The merry-go-round operator was walking the full circle of the ride to be sure each rider appeared to be old enough to ride unattended or had an adult beside them. One youngster stopped the man and asked, "What's this horse's name, sir?"

"They don't have names, they're just rides," he replied and moved along to check the rest of the riders.

The child looked up at her mother and said, "Well, I'm naming her Milly in honor of our mayor who got the rides here!" she said. Parents of little ones stood beside them, sometimes insisting on rides that didn't go up and down "until you're older. Those are for the bigger children." Some parents and adolescents who wanted to ride but thought they were too grown up for the animals were in the fancy gilded benches. The calliope was playing "The Man on the Flying Trapeze" when the operator called out, "Are all the riders ready?"

A chorus of "Giddy-up," "Let's go," "I *am* holding on tight, Mom" rang out, and the ancient machine rumbled into motion. The first day of the fair had begun.

It was close to nine thirty when Milly and her administrative team arrived. The loudspeaker boomed out across the entire fairgrounds. "Ladies and gentlemen, friends and neighbors, welcome to the annual Martin County Fair. Mayor Milly will officially start us off with a Citizen's Parade, where the Fancy Hats will be modeled and the youth with 4-H animals will lead their animals for all to see. The Antique Car and Truck Club will follow, and you all know Arthur Linden's steam tractor will end the parade. Get your popcorn and find a bench on the parade route, the procession is about to begin."

There had always been a friendly competition among the Ditzy Dozen in the pie contest, and most of the youngsters who had helped Wednesday with setup of the rides had animals to show as well. The rides brought extra excitement, and having Milly on the lot all day also added to the gaiety. Amanda had two pies to be judged, a cherry and an apple. Having given her girls strict instructions to check back with her every fifteen minutes, she found a bench under the grandstand and watched people mix and mingle. Jenny, who had a pie in the competition as well, spotted her.

"Hi, Amanda. Share the bench? I'm really about walked out, and today's just the first day."

"Hi, Jenny," Amanda said, scooting to one side to give Jenny room. "I know what you mean. The girls can't see it all fast enough, and they've already been on both rides twice."

"We're really lucky to have such great weather the first year we have rides. If it holds like it's supposed to, the rides will make enough money that we can probably have them back again next year."

"I'm pretty amazed at our little town these last few months. It seems like lots of good things have been happening." Amanda smiled. "I've had to watch my mouth not to say something on Ditzy Dozen night that might hurt Lucy's feelings, but I think a lot of it is because of Milly, and Arthur is doing more now that he's not mayor than he did when he was!"

Jenny laughed. "Yes, I know what you mean. She's such a sweet thing, and Arthur's not a bad type. Maybe the reason she's so quiet is because he isn't!"

"Do you have Jenny's Café Two here? It's become kind of a fixture at outdoor events since Milly's swearing-in ceremony," Amanda asked.

"Yes, it's set up over by the food trucks," Jenny replied. "I left Patsy at the café and hired two of the recent graduates to take care of the stand for three days. I'll check in on them from time to time, but I've known their parents forever. I'm sure they'll be fine."

Just then, Arthur's voice came over the PA system. "In just ten more minutes, the baked pie judging will begin. All you ladies with a pie in the contest should make your way over to section four under the grandstand to stand by your pies."

Jenny and Amanda looked at each other, stood, and with a forced energy they didn't feel, they headed to the pie contest. They grinned at each other, and Jenny said it first: "I hope you win, Amanda."

"I hope you win, Jenny," Amanda echoed back.

They watched as the judges looked over the pies, evaluating the appearance and eye appeal of each pie. They made comments and circled scoring levels on their evaluation sheets for appearance. Then they cut slices out of the pies, and each of the four judges got a slice of pie. They each took a bite, made more notes on their evaluation sheets, and took another bite. There were nodding heads, making sounds of "mmmm," and jotting more notes on the evaluation sheets. As the judges moved from one pie to the next, the announcer gave some information about each pie. "This cherry pie was made by Amanda Baker, who has the local hair salon in town. Most of you probably know Amanda. She says this is her grandmother's pie recipe. As a child, she would help her grandmother pick the cherries and learned to make her pie when she was only eight years old. She also has an apple and peach pie in the contest. Amanda says that making pies for her family is something she has always enjoyed."

The judges moved along to the next pie. Jenny gave Amanda a quick hug. "I'm sure your cherry pie will win," she said. "I was watching the judges' eyes as they made their notes. You make a really good cherry pie."

"Thanks, Jenny. I really do hope you win too. Your lemon meringue pie has been a favorite at the café ever since I can remember."

Saturday morning, there were large posters at each end of the grandstand announcing the winners of the previous day's contests. Amanda won with cherry pie, and Jenny won for lemon meringue. Lucy had knitted a beautiful sweater that won in the fiber arts competition. The big event on Saturday, besides the Decorated Hat Auction scheduled for six p.m., was Chicken Drop Bingo. Johnny Ray had brought a dozen chickens and a large floor had been enclosed with wire fencing, including a roof. At one end was a chicken coop with the chickens. On the large wooden floor, a five-column grid had been painted and repainted to be fresh each year. Each column had fifteen numbers, corresponding with the numbers that might be under the letters on the bingo cards. Visitors had bought bingo cards all day long, and at quarter to four, they began to gather at the perimeter of the wire enclosure. Arthur stood by the coop with the microphone. "Ladies and gentlemen, welcome to Chicken Drop Bingo. If you want to play in the first round, step up to one of the green wooden circles we've got around the coop and we'll begin. Once the chickens are released, Johnny Ray and I will keep a careful eye on the bingo floor, and we'll yell out any number that gets a chicken drop. Drops that land on a border too close to call will not be included. As we call out the numbers, mark your cards, and as soon as you get a bingo, holler out real loud, and we'll put the chickens back into the coop and validate your card. You can pick from any of the donated items over there in the prize booth. We'll hose down and go for another round as long as there are people here to play. You can play as many cards as you want when you're on deck, but at the end of each game, all cards are collected and can't be reused. We have to have at least ten players for a game to start. So, if you don't win this time, buy another card for only a dollar and play again. OK, let's go. Looks like we've got a player in every position, so Johnny Ray if you'll pull the doors up and let the chickens out, we'll get this adventure going."

It wasn't long before someone called out, "Look, one dropped on number fourteen." It only took about six minutes for the dozen chickens to drop enough for a winner. The game went on for two hours when the chickens were finally shooed back into the coop to be loaded onto Johnny Ray's truck and taken home.

By Saturday afternoon, the rides had paid their cost in ticket sales, and Milly's management team was delighted to see that the lines at the rides were no shorter into the evening. "That's money enough to pay Paul's line of credit at the bank and put some aside for next year," Ralph exclaimed. The others nodded. No one paid any particular attention to the man in jeans and a plaid western-style shirt who was in line for a pork chop on a stick.

Saturday evening's main event was the Decorated Hat Auction. In addition to the regular cakes and pies, this year would be the first year for such an auction. Arthur Linden, in his traditional role as spokesperson and general MC for the fair, strode up to the center of the stage and leaned into the microphone. "Ladies and gentlemen, it's time for the event you've waited two months for—the Ladies Decorated Hat Auction. Head for the grandstand now and get a seat up close. You'll want to see each one of these lovely hats. Bid on your favorite one, don't let somebody else get your favorite one! Remember, all the money raised goes to pay for the Ferris wheel and merry-go-round. If we raise enough money this year, we can put a deposit and guarantee our date on their route for next year. So bid on more than one hat!"

People were starting to fill the seats in front of the stage, and Arthur began his introductions. "Ladies and gentlemen, first we have Amanda Baker. She runs Bridgeford's hair salon. I think most of the ladies here know her. You can count on somebody who knows hair to know hats, and look at this one. This is hat number one, so if you want this one—all the bid sheets are on the foot of the stage—you can come down and put your name and your bid. Then watch to see if someone outbids you and bid again." He continued on, describing each hat, encouraging the crowd to bid. The line of ladies in hats was longer than anyone had expected—there were sixty-eight ladies in hats! The line started at the left end of the stage and had to keep scooting over to make room at the other end for all of the entries. Each of the ladies walked across the stage, did a little pirouette in the center, and then mingled with the crowd, encouraging folks to see the hat close up and bid on it. "Now you husbands should probably bid on your wife's hat, just so she knows you think it's the best. I know I'd best bid on Sally's if I want to go home tonight!"

After all the ladies had shown their hats on stage and mingled with the crowd for a while, Arthur took up the microphone again. "Last call for bids on the First Annual Decorated Hat Auction. Take one more look, and if you're not the high bidder on a hat you really want, make one more bid. We're picking up the bid sheets in ten minutes."

There was a flurry of people checking bid sheets, good-natured kidding, and compliments to all the ladies on their hats. Arthur picked up the bid sheets and strode to the stage. "Gather 'round, people. The auction is closed, and I have the winners right here." He waved the bid sheets in the air. "Ladies, if you'll all come up here and stand in numerical order, Amanda first, you can each present your hat to the winning bidder." The women all went to the stage steps, climbed, and crossed to stand behind Arthur in a line. "First, Amanda Baker's hat—hat number one—Hair Apparent. The winning bidder is John Baker, Amanda's husband, for $75. Let's have a round of applause for Hair Apparent." The audience applauded, and John's friends congratulated him. He went to the cashier's table, paid his bid, came up on stage, and Amanda handed him the hat.

The crowd applauded, and he promptly placed it on her head and gave her a kiss. When he lingered a little too long on the kiss, people were cheering him on, and he broke away and grinned. He leaned into the microphone and said, "Hey, folks, I just paid $75 for that hat. I should get a pretty good kiss for that!" He started to step away.

Arthur stopped him, held the microphone toward him, and said, "As the first winning bidder, do you have any special words for the audience?"

"I wanted to make sure it went to the prettiest lady at the fair," he responded.

Arthur took back the microphone as people clapped. "A wise man," he quipped. "A very wise man indeed."

Arthur continued to announce the winners, and one by one, the hats were bought and taken from the makers. As the last one finished, Arthur gave his closing announcement. "Ladies and gentlemen, the rides and booths and food court will continue to operate until eleven p.m. We'll need to be out of the way and off the grounds by midnight so the ride operators can pack up and head to their next stop. I do have a total of money raised on the Hat Auction. For sixty-eight hats, we raised $3,750. We will continue to get part of ticket sales until the rides close down. This has been a tremendous year for Bridgeford and Martin County, and while I haven't talked directly to the representatives of the mayor's office, I think it's safe to say we can have the rides back next year." A round of applause and cheers rang out as the crowd dispersed back out to the fairgrounds for more rides, midway games, and for some who had been there since morning, to head to the parking field to go home. The man in the western shirt watched the crowd leaving the grandstand area. He hadn't spoken to anyone except the occasional food vendor all day. He had observed everything, though. He had drifted through the fair unnoticed all weekend, and now he went to his car. No one noticed him as he drove off.

21

It was the last Saturday in June, and Milly's administrative management team had an air of celebration as they sat down for their usual Saturday morning breakfast. Ralph was a bit louder than usual, and Dan was more exuberant than he had been in a long time.

"Well, boys, you did it," Jenny poured their coffee and took their orders.

"We did, didn't we?" Johnny Ray said. "I would never have guessed it would get this far, but Milly's been really good for this town."

"And having rides at the fair was a real success. I think we can do this every year, as long as the energy for the fundraising keeps up," Steve said.

"Yes, and Amanda is selling three cherry pies a week here at Jenny's café!" Dan chimed in. "I think I'll just have to have some dessert with my breakfast today to celebrate."

Just then, a man they didn't recognize approached the table and said, "Excuse me, are you the administrative management team for the mule that won the election last spring?"

"Yes, we are," Ralph replied. "Pull up a chair and join us. We're going to have Milly's Mayor Meeting at noon, but if you have something you want to run by us in advance, you're welcome to join us here."

Johnny Ray and Steve pulled a nearby table up to extend their table and pulled up chairs. The stranger extended his hand. "I'm David Croslin. I'm from the secretary of state's office." He said this with an air of importance that didn't ring true as he sat at the end of the table. The four friends went suddenly silent as Jenny poured his coffee. "I need to talk to you boys about that election stunt you pulled."

Steve spoke first. "We were just having fun among ourselves. We never had any idea she would win."

Ralph was ready to defend his friends and spoke with an edge to his voice. "Milly got elected, and we're doing just fine here in Bridgeford. The town's doing better than it has in a long time. You boys at the state capital can just leave us alone."

"Well, that's the thing," Croslin said. "I can't just leave you alone. I'm going to have to disqualify Milly, and you're going to have to stop holding these meetings every Saturday."

Johnny Ray was never one to be told by a stranger what he had to do or not do. "We can meet any time we want. If other people from the town want to join us, there's nothing you can do to stop us. It's not a state issue. We're not breaking any laws. We're just a bunch of town citizens talking about what we'd like to see happen in our town. It's working for us, and we're not going to stop." He looked across at the other three for confirmation, and they were all nodding their support.

Dan spoke next. "Milly is my mule, and I can bring her to town if I want to. I checked with my nephew, and he assured me we're not doing anything illegal."

Croslin pushed his glasses up on his forehead. "Look, boys, I'm not here to cause trouble. I got a call from the secretary of state. Evidently, this is causing him some embarrassment because a TV station called to ask if a mule can be mayor. He sent me down here to check things out. Come Monday, I'm going to have to go to the local election commission and find out which one of you boys forged the affidavit of eligibility for her."

None of Milly's administrative management team said a word. They just looked at him in stony silence. Finally, Croslin stood up and took his plate and coffee over to a different table. Steve and

Ralph pulled the extra table back to its original place. Johnny Ray spoke first. "Well, I don't know what he thinks he can do. We can meet, the people who want to meet with us can do that. If we have Milly there, we don't need anyone's permission."

"And we've got more done in this town since Milly was elected than we have in the last twelve years. He can tell his secretary of state to go whistle up a stump for all I care." Ralph was still feeling a bit aggressive about it all.

Dan was calmer. After all, it was his nephew Jason who said no one could charge them with anything. "Well, let's just see how it plays out. What he doesn't know is the local election commissioner is the dad of the kids who first wanted the rides at the fair. I'll let him know after the Mayor's Meeting that this guy is in town. I don't think anything will come of it. That Croslin fella won't find any forgery because none of us filled out any affidavit of anything."

"I hope not," Johnny Ray said. "We don't need some bureaucrat from the capital messing with our town." The conversation turned to how they would keep the people who attended Milly's Mayor's Meeting from getting upset. By the time they'd finished their breakfast, and their cherry pie dessert, they had a plan.

By noon, a good-sized crowd had assembled at the bus station. Jenny had called Amanda, and the Ditzy Dozen had alerted their friends that it was important to be at Milly's Mayor's Meeting that afternoon. Their husbands had delayed the softball game to attend as well. There were close to one hundred citizens there when Milly was brought out.

Ralph called the meeting to order and raised his hands to begin to quiet the crowd. "Thank you all for coming today." People started shushing each other, and he continued, "We had great success last weekend with the fair, and we wanted to share the results of the fundraising and the rides. We want to ask the county fair board to stand up here with us. The town and the county worked together real well to make this a great event for our families." Six county fair board members stood, and the audience applauded. "We were able to pay off the loan to the bank with only $87 interest, thanks to Paul Fuller of First Security Bank for assisting with a line of credit for the deposit on the rides. We actually drew a larger crowd than we have in the last few years, and I think it was the rides that drew them in. The rides were out of here by Monday morning, and we went to check out Brian Douglass's fields to make sure there was no damage, and they were fine. Chet's grandson and his friends kept the place real neat and clean. There were no injuries, although one person did get lightheaded and had to sit in the first aid tent for a few minutes to get cooled off. All in all, it was a great fair."

As applause started to spread through the audience, someone shouted, "Mayor Milly was an inspiration to us," and another one yelled over the growing applause, "Three cheers for Mayor Milly Day!"

Dan and Ralph looked at each other. "Wrap it up before that Croslin guy does anything," Dan hissed.

Ralph raised his hands again. "Well, we're glad you all enjoyed the fair, and we'll certainly try to have the rides again next year." The applause died down as he spoke and people were listening again. "That's about all the news we have for you today, so why don't we all have something to eat from Jenny's Outdoor Café here on the lot." He started to lead Milly back to the lot where her trailer was, and Croslin stood up.

"Wait a minute. I have something to bring to the attention of the town residents."

The four friends looked at each other, didn't say anything, but the few who had risen to leave sat back down. Croslin strode to the front of the crowd and turned to face them. When he spoke, his voice was loud and commanding. "I'm David Croslin, and I represent the office of the secretary of state. I've tried to have a meeting with your county election commissioner, but he's not been in his office and doesn't return his messages. So, I came here in person today and spoke with the mayor's administrative management team at the café this morning. I let them know that Milly has been disqualified as mayor because—"

The residents all started speaking at once. "We elected her" and "She got more votes than the only other candidate" and "Arthur has acknowledged he didn't win," and it began to get heated when the shouts turned to "Go back to wherever you came from" and "We don't need you to tell us how to run our town."

Steve was always level-headed in a crisis. He stepped up to stand beside Croslin. "Wait, people, wait a minute. It's not our nature in Bridgeford to be rude to visitors. I'm sure there's a way we can work this out." The shouting faded, and he continued, "Please sit back down and let's see how we can work this out." He turned to Croslin. "David," he said, "this town has not had any problems with Milly as mayor, and she has brought our town together to accomplish a lot. I think you should be able to make an exception for us. We're not affecting anything else in any other town, and good things are happening here."

"I understand that," Croslin responded. "But this has got all the way to the capital, and the secretary of state is getting some pressure. It's making a mockery of the democratic process, and we can't let our state get that reputation. It's really not legal. Any write-in candidate that wins must have the election results certified, and part of that certification is to have a filed affidavit of candidacy, which Milly did not file, and even if she had, it would have had to assert that she was a registered voter in the country, which she isn't and can't become one. So, it's really out of my hands. She is officially disqualified, and the runner-up, Arthur Linden, is the legal winner of the election."

Arthur stood up. "What if I refuse?"

"Then the town will have to hold another election and bear that expense. And the winner will have to be certified as a registered voter to be eligible. I'm sorry, folks, but that's the law, and I have to enforce it." He paused a moment, then softened his tone some. "Look, folks," he said, "I understand what you're thinking here. No individual broke any law by voting for Milly. The fundraising and other good things that have happened since the election are commendable. Getting the rides here, holding the Decorated Hat Auction, getting the new mulch in the park, all that is fine. I'm really not here to shut down the town's engagement in solving your problems and bringing good things to Bridgeford. However, it remains that the town does not have a legally elected mayor, and that's a problem. If Arthur Linden refuses to serve as runner-up, you have to have a legally elected mayor."

The crowd started to mumble, and it threatened to get loud again. Steve spoke up. "How much time can you give us to figure out a solution?"

"I need to get on the road and return to the capital. It's getting late. I can give you until this time next week to let me know what you're going to do. But you have to do something."

With that, Croslin reached out to shake Steve's hand in a gesture of goodwill. Steve shook his hand and said, "We'll figure out something and let you know. Certified letter postmarked no later than next Saturday, OK?"

"That's fine. I'll let the secretary of state know we will be expecting that letter." He tried to put the stern official tone back in his voice, but it wasn't quite there.

Croslin walked to his car, and as soon as he was out of earshot, Steve held up his hands to quiet the crowd again. "Folks, I think I have an idea. Let's wait until we see Croslin's car drive off, and maybe we can solve this right now."

Someone called out, "I just saw him turn onto Oak and head toward the highway."

Steve looked at Ralph and Dan and Johnny Ray, who all nodded. If Steve had an idea, it was more than they had to offer.

"Arthur, are you still here?" Steve called out.

"I'm here," Arthur responded.

"Well, Milly's administrative team has a favor to ask of you."

"I'm listening," Arthur replied.

"Since the election commission guy seems to think you won as runner-up, would you be willing to be the "official mayor of record" in the state offices, and we can continue to have Mayor's Meetings here on Saturday, and you can appoint the four of us"—he swept his hand to indicate Dan, Ralph, and Johnny Ray—"we can still be the mayor's administrative management team at the same pay we've been getting, which is nothing, and we can hold Mayor's Meetings in your absence. You'd be welcome to attend, you can participate as much as you want, and we can hold the Mayor's

Meetings pretty much the same way we have for the last few months. If anyone asks, your name is on the records as being the official legal mayor."

"That sounds like a solution to me," Arthur said. "I liked the parades and such, but having everybody bring me their complaints was not what I enjoyed all that much. You know I farm a good-sized acreage, and having to solve somebody else's problem when I'd already worked hard to run the farm, well, I guess I just lost my energy for it, and I guess it showed. I'm happy to support Milly's administrative management team."

Steve quickly corrected him. "Well, I think in the letter to the election commission, we have to be careful not to mention Milly, and just call it the mayor's administrative management team. This sound OK as a way to satisfy the state legally and keep things the way we want them? Is this a good compromise?"

Most people cheered; Arthur was nodding his head. Then someone shouted out, "Well, Milly's still mayor until you send that letter. We have to ask her."

Ralph grinned from ear to ear. He loved this town. "Of course, that's right." He turned to Milly, who looked pretty complacent and unlikely to move. "And just to reward her, I'd like to ask all of you to come up here and get a handful of hay to feed her as a reward when she votes." Johnny Ray moved to stand close to her rear flank, in case he was to lose his balance and start to fall and have to steady himself against her. Folks in the front of the gathering grabbed some hay from the bales around the lot.

"Milly, do you agree to relinquish your official title as mayor but continue to show up here on Saturday mornings to observe the mayor's administrative team as they assist Arthur Linden in his official duties?"

The crowd watched intently. Someone held the hay right in front of Milly's mouth. She took a step forward to nibble the offering. The crowd started counting: "Ten, nine, eight, seven, six..." Milly reached for a bit more hay. Arthur had his hand the closest, and he pulled back just a bit as she stretched her neck out for the bite. He backed up, and she stepped forward and got a good mouthful of hay. The crowd applauded and cheered.

Dan stepped forward. "Thank you, Arthur." They shook hands. "We'll get that letter off to the capital on Monday."

Arthur smiled. "Don't thank me, thank Mayor Milly."

Discussion Guide

1. Many stories are written simply to entertain, and I hope this accomplishes that goal. But I had a second, stronger need to write this, with a specific message. What is the overall message of the story?

2. Often stories are the tale of something that goes wrong, then it gets fixed. When did you first suspect something would go awry? What specifically do you think went awry? Why did it happen? Before you had read this story, would you have voted for Milly? Why or why not? What would you do differently now?

3. Why do you think Arthur wanted to be mayor? Did his childhood with his sister Lucy influence any of his behaviors later in life? Why do you think Arthur took a picture of him to the print shop that was from years earlier?

4. What do you think of the Mayor's Administrative Team? While not illegal to encourage a write-in vote, was it morally or ethically

wrong to trick the town? Did it do any damage? If so, to whom?

5. What do you think would have happened if Milly had not been confirmed as mayor? Would Arthur have changed in any way? Was Arthur different in any way by the end of the story?

6. There are many examples of good team behavior that is intentional and conscious. A few examples might include team sports or competition barbershop singing. Activities where success depends on the team acting in the best interest of the team rather than the individual are often deliberately focused on supporting all members of the team.

    A. Would you describe the four friends in the café as team behavior?

    B. Would you describe the town's reaction to the election of Milly as team behavior? Why or why not?

    C. What would you have done if you had been one of the four friends in the café?

D. What would you have done after the election if you had been a citizen in the town of Bridgeford?

7. When Johnny Ray is in the barber shop, Sam says, "One person can't make a difference." What do you think about Sam's statement? Do you have any examples of when one person did something and it made a difference? Have you ever had the opportunity to be one person who made a difference? Do you know anyone who has? What do you think motivated them?

8. On election night, when the results are in, the announcer says there are 1,433 registered voters and 702 votes. Why do you think the author decided to have less than half of the registered voters in the results? Why didn't Milly's campaign result in a larger turnout? Do you think there will be a larger turnout at the next mayoral election?

9. When the four friends decide to build the stage for the swearing-in ceremony, Dan is reluctant to have city money involved in their effort. He is the reluctant one when they first

wanted to promote Milly. Is Dan the "grown-up in the room" in this group of four friends? Is Steve the natural leader? How do you think roles emerge in groups of friends?

About the Author

Dorothy Ramsey graduated from Southwest Missouri State University (go, Bears!) in 1980 with a double major in creative and technical writing. She then got caught in the corporate rat race, and it took her thirty years to escape! It took that long to figure out the rats always win. All that time, her husband was saying, "Why don't you just write your stories instead of telling me about them?" She is now semiretired, and semiconsulting, working from home. She says that reasons to be self-employed and work from home include shorter commute, better coffee, flexible hours, and every day is "Take Your Cat to Work" day. An added benefit of this work arrangement is that there is time available to dedicate to her stories. So she did! *Milly for Mayor* is the first of six stories under construction to be finished, and she can't wait to finish the next one. She lives in Lincoln, Nebraska, with Smokie Girl, a lynx point Siamese cat, and her dreams.

CPSIA information can be obtained
at www.ICGtesting.com
Printed in the USA
LVHW030810240821
695930LV00002B/10